didn't mean to love you

serendipitous love series book two

christina c jones

Didn't Mean To Love You

Copyright © 2014 Christina C. Jones

chapter
one

Vivienne

THIS WASN'T ANYTHING THAT COULDN'T BE FIXED with strong drinks and good company.

At least, that's what I told myself as I took the longest, hottest shower I could stand, then dressed in jeans, a sweater, and low-heeled boots, pulling my mass of curls into a messy bun on top of my head.

Less than thirty minutes after a breakup that would have paralyzed me in my early twenties, I was bouncing down the steps of my building into the brisk autumn night. I pulled out the earbuds nearly as soon as I put them in. Destiny's Child singing *Is She the Reason* in my ear wasn't the mood I needed to be in. It's not that I wasn't mad — I was *pissed* — but the last thing I was about to do was dwell on a man who didn't want me. At least not until the wee hours of the morning, when I was alone in my bed and *had* to face it. For now... loud music and loud friends.

"Yo, Viv!"

My steps faltered as a familiar voice called my name. It was a Friday night, but the dropping temperatures drove the usual crowds inside, instead of loitering on the sidewalks like they did in the warmer months. When I turned around, I got a clear view of Carter as he stepped out of the storefront I'd just passed.

His barbershop, Fresh Cuts, was a few doors down from my chocolate shop, Guilty Pleasures. I saw him around often, but it wasn't until I moved to a new building in walking distance of my store that I got the pleasure of *meeting* him. One day I stepped out of my apartment and right into six feet and four inches of *have-mercy,* in a black tank top and grey basketball shorts, his muscles dripping with sweat. Rich brown skin the color of roasted pecans, wide shoulders, bright, cheerful eyes, lush lips, and dark, well-groomed shoulder-length locs — he was the kind of stuff naughty dreams were made of. He smiled, asked if I was okay, and a few minutes later, I discovered that *he* was the person who woke me up every morning with Kanye West blasting through my bedroom wall.

We didn't become friends, not exactly. Or maybe we were, in an *"I would ride you until we both passed out, regained conscious, then do it all over again if I didn't have a man"* kind of way. Out of respect for Darren, whose eyes had nearly popped out of their sockets when he emerged up the stairs to my third floor apartment and saw me standing in front of it talking to my sweaty, fresh-off-the-basketball-court neighbor, I maintained a friendly distance. In retrospect, that was completely ridiculous because Darren had a *fiancé now*, a woman he had to have been dating at the same time we were... doing whatever we were doing. I'm not even sure what that was anymore.

"Hello Carter," I said, trying to pull a bit of cheerfulness into my voice as I took a few steps closer to him. He finished locking up his shop, then turned to me and smiled, sending instant warmth rushing through me. As he approached, looking delicious as always in a royal blue sweater, with his locs pulled back from his face, his eyes narrowed and he stopped, scrutinizing me from head to toe.

"What's going on with you?"

I frowned, then shrugged, suddenly self-conscious under his careful inspection. "Nothing."

Carter raised an eyebrow, taking the last few steps to put him barely a foot in front of me. "It's definitely not nothing."

"Because you know me so well?"

He grinned. "Well enough to know that your whole vibe is off. I mean, I didn't even realize you *owned* solid clothes. I've never seen you in less than four colors and you're standing in front of me in dark jeans, black sweater, and black boots."

"I am a thirty-year-old woman, Carter. My wardrobe should reflect that. Not a teeny-bopper trying to renew the grandeur of her youth. Everybody has to grow up, right?" I asked, my cheeks flushed from realizing he had been paying so much attention to me.

A smile played at the corners of his mouth as he shook his head. "So, in other words, you just don't wanna talk about it. That's cool," he said, cocking his head to the side as he surveyed me again. "Where you headed?"

"Down to Roman's," I said, nodding my head toward the coffee shop on the corner. "For a much-needed drink."

"Mind if I tag along?"

"The sidewalk is public space."

Carter's eyes went wide, and he chuckled as he began walking beside me. "*Damn*, Frenchy, you are *cold* today."

I stopped, glancing around the nearly-empty sidewalk. "Frenchy is... *me*? You are calling me Frenchy *why*?"

He smiled. "You've got that little sexy accent, so that's what I'm gonna call you."

I blushed, but didn't address the "sexy" comment. "I don't have an accent."

"Frenchy, you've got an accent."

"I do *not*. I used to, but I am very Americanized now. I *barely* have an accent."

Carter stared at me for a moment, the corners of his mouth twitching as he tried not to laugh.

"What is so funny?" I asked, crossing my arms over my chest.

"*You*," he said, finally giving in with a chuckle. "You sound like goddamned Pepe Le Pew, talking about you don't have an accent."

I gasped, a little bit horrified by that comparison before I burst into laughter myself, giggling until tears rolled down my face. "The *skunk*, Carter? You're comparing me to a *skunk*?"

"Just the accent, I swear. And you're fine as hell, so it's sexy."

My eyes went wide. "Oh, I'm pretty, so it is okay that I sound like a cartoon skunk with a *terrible* accent?"

"*Exactly.*"

Narrowing my eyes, I tried my best to hold it together, but laughter won over again. "How did you do that?" I asked, when I finally regained my composure.

"Do what?"

I shook my head, using my thumbs to wipe stray tears from my face. "I don't know... I sure as hell did not feel like laughing when I walked out of my apartment."

He shrugged. "Hell, I don't know. I'm just used to seeing a smile on your face. That's *you*, always grinning or laughing about something." He stopped, with his hand on the door to enter Urban Grind. I could already feel the beat of the music, smell the unique mixture of coffee and hookah smoke permeating the air near the entrance as Carter stepped closer. "You *sure* you okay?"

There was a concern in his eyes that made my heart race, and made me wonder just how "off" I looked. I tore my gaze away from his as I nodded. "I'm fine, Carter. Really."

I felt his eyes on me for another moment longer before he pulled the door open, surrounding us with a blast of warmth from inside. "Come on," he said, grabbing my hand to pull me in.

This was my first time ever *really* touching Carter, aside from literally bumping into him every once in a while at home. A little part of me hoped it wouldn't be the last, because electric warmth was circulating from my hand to his as he led me through the crowd, straight to where my friend — and fellow neighborhood business owner— Eddie was sitting, flanked by a couple of the artists from his tattoo and piercing parlor, DistInk'd.

At first, Eddie's eyes lit up when he saw me, but his expression shifted to barely veiled disgust as he scanned my wardrobe. "What the fuck is this boring shit you're *wearing*?" he asked, standing to give me a hug.

I rolled my eyes. "What is wrong with what I am wearing? And why are you *men* commenting on it?" I said, glancing between him and Carter.

Carter raised his hands in front of him. "Hey, I was just mentioning it because it wasn't how I'm used to seeing you. I wasn't complaining." He shot me a smile as he headed to the bar.

"*I'm* complaining," Eddie said, turning my face toward his. "Why are you dressed like you're about to perform a mime act?"

"I thought my outfit was chic..."

Eddie scoffed. "Maybe on another girl, but on *you*, Little Miss Technicolor... you look like you're in mourning... so I'm gonna guess you saw that Instagram post." He tugged me by the hand, ushering his companions to the other side of the booth so we could sit down. "You wanna talk about it?"

I took a deep breath, opened my mouth to speak, then decided against it. I was *not* supposed to dwelling on him, I was supposed to be getting tipsy and having fun. I looked Eddie right in the eyes as I shook my head, hoping that he would leave it alone.

"Okay... we don't have to talk about it... *yet*. But you *are* gonna tell me what's up with you and the barber."

Dropping my gaze, I tried to fight the little smile that threatened to spread across my lips. "What about him?"

"So," Eddie said, smirking as he leaned closer. "Are you *really* about to act like you didn't walk in here holding hands with *Fine Ass Carter?*"

Fine Ass Carter.

That was the nickname that Eddie, Simone and I had given him. I actually felt a little twinge of jealousy when Carter started pursuing Simone a few months ago, which was ridiculous, because I was dating Darren. She and I had just met, so there was no way she could have known about my illicit crush. But, she was way too immersed in Roman to give Carter much steam anyway, and when I accidentally outed myself, after she and Roman were officially dating, she actually gave her "blessing" on a connection between Carter and I.

"Where is Simone?" I asked, trying to deflect the conversation to more neutral ground. I didn't want to talk about Carter, or the fact that my hand was *still* tingling from his touch.

"Home. You know she's still on the outs with Roman because Lusty Leah is still at his apartment. But... don't change the subject. Are you and Carter—?"

"Doing anything that involves our genitals? No." I glanced over his head at a man and woman whose eyes kept lingering at our table. "Looks like you've got some admirers."

Smiling, Eddie shot a subtle grin over his shoulder, then turned back to me. "I think you're right." He picked up his drink from the table, finishing it in one gulp. "I'll talk to you later, Viv."

I watched, amused, as Eddie — who was an equal opportunity lover — shoved his hands into his pockets and sauntered over to the couple with a casual pace. Eddie was a handsome guy, with shoulder-length locs as well groomed as Carter's, deep ebony skin, and even blacker ink lines covering both of his sinewy arms. I could pinpoint the exact moment he charmed his way into their bed. A head thrown back in laughter, a lingering touch, eyes that said "Let's get out of here"... at least one of us wouldn't be going to bed lonely.

Across the room, Carter was getting similar body

language from a Poetic-Justice type with waist length braids and a big smile. I ignored the stitch of jealousy that tugged at my chest and headed to the bar for the drink I'd left my apartment for, and *still* hadn't gotten.

"Roman!" I shouted across the counter, getting his attention. He perked up a little when he saw me, and headed my way, but I could practically feel the melancholy oozing off him. "You look terrible." I smiled after I said it, hoping to get one back in return for my teasing, but the one he gave me was forced.

"Thanks for the compliment," he said dryly, crossing his arms over his chest. "What can I get you?"

"Black Russian. Double."

He lifted an eyebrow, but nodded, then turned to fix the drink for me. "So...," he said, pulling a bottle of Stolichnaya vodka, then the Urban Grind house coffee liqueur from the cabinet on the wall. "You talked to Simone lately?"

"She is fine, Roman. She just needs a little time. *Chill*," I said as he poured the two ingredients for my drink into an ice-filled shaker. I smiled again as he turned to me, poured the finished drink into a glass, then slid it to me on a napkin. "Simone is crazy about you. She is not going anywhere... as long as you get Leah out of your apartment."

That time, he smiled back — a *real* one — before he turned to tend to another customer, leaving me to nurse my drink alone.

So much for good company.

But at least the drink was good. Strong, but good.

I was just about finished with it, and starting to retreat into my emotions when Carter approached. This time, he didn't say anything, just took a seat beside me as my eyes clouded with tears.

"I think I am going to head home," I said carefully, not wanting the hitch in my voice to give away my feelings. He nodded, eyes slightly narrowed as he tried to get me to make eye contact. I avoided his gaze, but shook my head when he asked if I minded if he walked with me. I wasn't ready to be alone... not just yet.

Outside, the crisp autumn air cooled the warm flush that the Russian vodka had brought to my skin. It was sobering, a little, and I couldn't decide if that was good or not as Carter caught me by the hand again. It took a lot more than a single — well, double — drink to get me intoxicated, but my lips definitely felt loose as we walked along, hand in hand. The last thing I wanted to do was spill my heart out to a guy that, as far as I knew, could very well think he was going to end up in my bed tonight. That thought made me give a half-hearted attempt to tug my hand away from his. He released it, but gave me a slightly confused smile that made me wonder if I was just being silly.

"So... chocolate," he said, pushing his hands into his pockets as he broke the silence between us. "How in the world did you end up in *that* business?"

I sighed, glad for a seemingly neutral topic, even though the story— if I told it *all*— was melodramatic in its own right. I decided on the non-theatrical version. "My family," I said, clasping my hands behind me as we walked. "The Lamberts... we... or *they*, I should say, are one of the largest providers of fair-trade chocolate in the world. *Largest*, period, in France."

"Fair-trade?"

I nodded. "Yes. Meaning that there is no slave labor involved. Fairly paid employees, humane working conditions, conflict-free source ingredients, and so forth."

"Sounds pretty cool."

"It is." I smiled. "My parents... um, my mother is African-American, an expat. She went to Paris to expand her education, and somehow fell in love with my father. He is multi-racial— Afro-French and white French, and they are *truly* a case of "opposites attract". They both joke that my mother got *all* of the liberal, while my father has all of the logical. Individually, they both came from "good" families — from money, to put it plainly. But, they are very big on philanthropy, humanitarianism... that sort of thing."

"They sound cool. Are you pretty close with them?"

I paused to let him open the door to our building, a little caught off guard by how seemingly fast the walk had gone. "Yes," I replied when we were inside, beginning the three-flight trek up the stairs to our floor. "Well... my mother, yes. Father, not so much. I do not see them as often as I would like anymore, but... things happen." Focusing on the handrail, I hoped that avoiding his gaze would send the message that I'd said as much as I wanted, but he persisted.

"Why don't you see them? They don't live close?"

"No," I shook my head. "They are in France still."

"Oh. So... you came by yourself?"

"In a manner of speaking."

Carter chuckled as we finally reached our floor. "What does that even mean?"

Sighing, I fished my keys from my back pocket, then leaned against my door. "Um... when I was 24... just about ready to buckle down and start a life of my own... I got in trouble."

He lifted an eyebrow. "*Trouble*. As in... baby trouble?"

"*No*," I laughed. "And nothing illegal, just... *trouble*. Embarrassed my parents pretty bad, so instead of a position in France, they shipped me off to the United States, and put me to work in one of the shops."

"Wow," Carter said, leaning against his own door. You got *in trouble* enough that your super liberal French mom sent you away. I'm.... *not* surprised," he finished with a teasing chuckle.

"Oh whatever." I shook my head, looking down at the slightly scuffed toes of my boots as I traced a line of the deep brown hardwood floor. "But yes... I came to the US seven years ago. I finally earned my own shop two years ago."

"Earned?"

"Yes. My parents are generous, but they *give* me nothing, not now that I'm an adult. I had to submit a business plan, budgets, all of that. Convince my parents that a more youthful, modern chocolate shop could be a success. My fancy Ecole Normale Supérieure education came in handy, I guess."

"I have no idea what that is, but it sounds seductive."

I laughed, shaking my head as I brought my gaze back up to meet his. "Ecole Normale Supérieure — ENS, Paris. The university I attended... nothing titillating about it."

"Oh, I disagree," he said, grinning as he lifted a finger. "I happen to think that a gorgeous woman with an education is *very* sexy."

Our gazes held for a moment, and something... perhaps a deep, mutual attraction, passed between us until I finally tore my eyes away, clearing my throat. "Um... have you been into the shop before? I am sure I would have seen you if you had."

"I haven't, actually," he admitted, with a slight grimace. "I don't have a big sweet tooth."

"Oh. Too bad."

"Yeah."

A few moments passed with neither of us saying anything. I don't know what was holding *him* in the hallway, but I was in no hurry to be alone with thoughts that would surely turn to Darren.

"Well... I'll see you later Frenchy."

I smiled at his insistent use of the nickname he'd given me as I turned to open my door. "Bye Carter."

"Hey," he said, eyes shining with mischief as he poked his head out just before he closed his door behind him.

"Yeah?"

"You *don't* sound like the skunk."

I rolled my eyes as I laughed, pushing open my door. "Gee, thanks Carter."

"You're welcome. Good night."

"Good night."

As soon as I locked the door, overwhelming loneliness swept over me, bringing a fresh wave of tears to my eyes. They fell on the aluminum bat I'd tossed onto the couch earlier, bringing a layer of shame to merge with my seclusion. I pulled a bottle of water from the fridge, draining it to soothe my suddenly dry mouth.

Engaged. Darren was *engaged*, and even though I'd seen it with my own eyes, I could still barely believe it.

—

I couldn't breath.

A wave of cold settled over my skin, causing goosebumps to spring up on my arms as I shook my head, shutting down my Instagram app and opening it again, knowing that I'd misread the caption on the picture filling my screen. No way I was seeing that right.

But... Eddie would not have sent this to me if he wasn't sure. And... there it was again, with 313 "likes".

"The future Mr. & Mrs. Blake. I LOVE black love! So happy for these two! I know this wedding is gonna be thebomb.com! #BlakeEngagementTurnUp."

Engagement... what?

What?

I let the tablet fall to the floor with a clatter as I stood, walking on shaky legs to the bathroom to splash cool water on my face.

Getting... married.

"Awww, congrats Kelly and Darren! I'll be on the lookout for my invite! #blacklove"

"Whhaaaa! Girl you got Darren to "put a ring on it"?! I see you!"

"Look at my big sister and future bro in law! Beautiful black couple!"

"Kelly, girrrrrllll he FAHN! And that ROCK?! Gon' head then! Congratulations!"

"Darren reunited with his queen, how beautiful!"

"Glad to see you guys put the foolishness behind you to focus on your love. Congratulations, this is wonderful!"

It went on like that, for upwards of fifty comments,

congratulating them on their engagement. Kelly and Darren.
Kelly and Darren. My Darren.

You mean... *her* Darren?

I tossed the tablet in the general direction of the coffee table,
not really caring if it landed there or not. In another second, I
would have launched it across the room.

Married.

I was sitting at home, wondering why he hadn't returned
a call or text in two days and this man was getting married?
Heat rushed through me, and my heart throbbed in my ears as
I snatched up my purse, emptying the contents on my counter to
find my cell phone. I was shaking as I unlocked the phone,
found his number in my favorite contacts, then hit the "call"
button. A few seconds later, I pulled the phone away from my
ear, staring in awe at the screen as his voice, dry and formal,
directed me to leave a message.

He'd declined my call and sent me to voicemail.

Okay.

O. Kay.

I jabbed angrily at the screen as I wrote out a message and
hit send.

"You are getting married now, Darren? WHAT IS
GOING ON?"

Pacing the kitchen as I waited for a response, I tried unsuc-
cessfully to calm myself down.

"You're stalking me or something now, Viv?
What's going on with YOU? - Darren."

Did he just... I know he didn't say ... breathe, Viv. Just...
breathe. Breathe. Breathe.

"Nobody is stalking you. Stop it. My friend is
apparently friends with a friend of one of YOUR

friends. They reposted a picture you were tagged in, my friend sent me a link, and there YOU are, grinning in some woman's face while she lugs around that big-assed ring. I'm confused."

"I don't know what you want me to say to you. I mean... it's not like we were official or anything. - Darren"

It's not like we were...

I slammed my fists on the counter, fighting back the urge to scream before I picked up the phone again to respond.

"When has that ever been an issue, Darren? No labels, remember? We both know what this was, what we were doing. Are you telling me now that we were just... screwing? After the promises you've made, you can actually say to me "it's not like we were official"?! "

"Calm down with that shit, Viv. We were just... talking, you know? I didn't mean anything by that, it's just... the stuff you're supposed to say. You didn't think we were serious, did you? - Darren"

"Are YOU serious right now, Darren? You can't be. No. You're not serious about this."

"That's just the stuff you're supposed to say."

Is that what he was doing? Was he actually telling me that he was just saying what he needed to for me to... for me to do what? He couldn't pretend that what we were doing was just sex. We'd cuddled together, bought groceries, shared our fears and dreams, we had keys to each other's places! But he wanted to say we weren't serious? And he couldn't give me the courtesy of talking to me?

What the hell was he trying to pull? Pretending that he hadn't talked about a future together with me. A house. Kids.

Darren was supposed to be the "safe" choice. A good man, with a good job, who — as my mother advised — cared for me more than I cared for him. It didn't matter that he did nothing for my soul, the bare minimum for my body, and scarcely more than that for my mind. He was the kind of man who would not break your heart.

"We had a good time, Viv. Made a few memories. Let's just leave it at that and move on. - Darren."

Leave it at that and move on.

"Wow, Darren. That's where we are? That's what I get from you now? I guess this answers my question about the distance over the last few weeks. But you were here two days ago. We made love... two days ago. You could have just told me you did not want me anymore. This is how I had to find out you were ENGAGED?"

"Viv... I'm sorry. I'm blocking this number. Don't call/text again. -Darren."

What!? Blocking my number? As if I was harassing him by trying to figure how the hell we went from whispered words of love to him being engaged — to somebody else — in two days?

Okay.

He wanted to treat me like I was nothing, like I was a problem to be solved, okay. I could oblige that. I stomped into my bedroom to pull on a pair of sweatpants and a tee shirt, both his. Lacing my feet into a pair of Nikes, I glanced up at the full length mirror across the room. A little voice whispered "what are you doing, Vivienne?" into my ear, but I shook my head, clearing the thought from my mind.

I shoved my cell phone into my pocket, grabbed my keys and wallet from the discarded contents of my purse on the counter, and headed for the door. I stopped by my hall closet for the aluminum bat I kept there in case of an emergency. This certainly qualified.

With the bat resting on my shoulder, I pulled my door closed behind me and locked it.

Then... I couldn't take another step. An overwhelming mix of guilt, shame, and anger had me paralyzed as I stood there in the hall, simultaneously trying to convince and talk myself out of going to Darren's house and destroying everything I could find — Darren included. Let him explain that *to his pretty little fiancé.*

But how crazy did I look, walking around in sweats with a bat? How would my mugshot look after I got myself arrested? How would I explain this nonsense to my father? I could see it now, "Local chocolatier Vivienne Lambert was arrested this evening for assault and battery, destruction of property, and in a disturbing turn of events, forcibly removing the testicles of her former lover, Darren Blake."

I cringed.

This was stupid.

Shaking my head, I re-entered my apartment, tossing the bat onto the couch before I sat down. Not giving myself a chance to settle into sadness, I hopped up and got in the shower, determined that I wasn't going to wallow in misery. I was going to let Eddie get me drunk, and dance this mood away.

—

But now, I had to make a choice. Alone, in my bed, no distractions, I had to decide if I wanted to unpack the emotional baggage of finding out that someone who I really thought I had a future with... saw it with somebody else.

No.

No, I didn't.

Despite the many privileges afforded to me in my life, the luxury of a guarded heart was something I'd never been granted. I gave it freely, without reservation, but I would just as easily take it back, after doing my usual work of burying my heartache.

That's what I wanted to do now.

I wanted to pack it away, and never address it again, just like every other failed relationship before it.

I wanted to pretend it never happened.

So... I did.

chapter
two

Vivienne

"SO... CARTER ASKED ABOUT YOU."

I lifted an eyebrow, but didn't otherwise respond. Schooling my features into an impassive mask, I ignored Simone's probing stare as I uncorked the bottle of wine.

"Specifically, about your relationship status."

Shoot.

I wasn't expecting *that*. My hand slipped, and I nearly dropped the bottle, catching it just before it hit the counter and spilled everywhere. Carefully placing it on the counter, I turned to glare at Simone, who was barely containing a smile. "Are you happy?" I asked, pulling the wine glasses in front of me.

"That depends on why just the *mention* of Carter has you all... butter-fingered." She raised her eyebrows, nodding impatiently like she was waiting for me to divulge some deep secret, but it wasn't happening — mostly because there *was* no deep secret. Only two days had passed since my breakup — if you could call it that — with Darren, and there hadn't been any great strides in my relationship with Carter.

Not that I was *looking* for progress in my relationship with Carter.

Not that I *had* a relationship with Carter.

"This is *your* damned fault," I said, pointing an accusing finger at Simone, who laughed in response. "It is not funny, you've got my head all messed up now."

"Like you and Eddie did to me the first night we met?"

Simone smiled sweetly, tilting her head to the side as if she were daring me to offer a rebuttal. I opened my mouth to do just that, then quickly closed it when I couldn't think of one, because she was absolutely right.

"Wait a minute," I said, raising a finger as something occurred to me. "*I* was the one trying to ease your nerves, it was really *Eddie* saying all of that inappropriate stuff to you about Roman's... equipment."

"Damned traitor."

I cringed as Eddie's voice carried into the kitchen as he turned the corner from using the bathroom. He took a seat at the bar beside Simone, reaching to grab a handful of cheese cubes from the bowl I'd placed on the counter.

"Isn't she?" Simone asked, playfully sticking out her tongue at me before snagging a toasted baguette slice. "And she's trying to change the subject, really."

The corners of Eddie's mouth pulled up into a smirk. "The subject? What are we talking about?"

"Nothi—"

"We're talking about the fact that gorgeous, gainfully employed, college educated but still maintained a little 'hood swagger, *Fine Ass Carter*... asked about Vivienne's relationship status," Simone said, talking over me.

"Oh *really* now?" Eddie's smirk spread into a grin. "Just

what kind of roots did you put on the barber after you left Urban Grind with him the other night? I told you they walked in holding hands, right?" he asked Simone.

Her mouth dropped open. "*No*, you did not, and *she* didn't either." Simone turned to me, eyes wide as she reached for another slice of bread. "You told us *all* about Darren's silly ass and the breakup, but nothing about you getting cozy with Carter, who you've *been* crushing on. You go from barely wanting to be in the same room with the man so you don't jump his bones, to holding his hand? Get to talking, missy."

"There is *nothing* to talk about," I insisted, shaking my head as I began to pour the wine. "Why are you all pushing so hard on this anyway?"

"Because Darren was *wack*." Eddie reached forward, grabbing the first glass I poured. "You need somebody with some... swagger."

"And you think *Carter* is the one?" I poured the second glass, lifting it to drink in one gulp at the prospect of *that*. "Carter isn't the type for a long commitment. He's more the type to get you... ad*dick*ted."

Eddie lowered his glass, giving me a slight scowl. "I don't see the problem."

Rolling my eyes, I proceeded to refill my glass. "So you are suggesting I do what... have a one night stand with him?"

"I'm *suggesting* you get your back broken in... you can call it what you want."

"*Eddie*," Simone interjected, "Does it have to always be about sex with you?"

"Not at all," Eddie replied. "I just know that great sex is part of a great relationship, so I encourage checking the merchandise as soon as possible. I mean, look at you and Roman. I told you he was probably *slanging* that thang, and I see I was right, cause you're still around."

"Eddie!"

"*What*?" he asked, eyes wide as though he was confused about why he was being scolded. "The man walks like his dick is heavy, anybody with eyes can see that. So Simone, I'm right about it, aren't I?"

"Umm... I don't think Roman would really appreciate me discussing his penis size."

Eddie lifted an eyebrow. "*Simone.*"

"He would *kill* me."

Eddie rolled his eyes, then took another swig from his glass. "Okay, Okay. I understand you want to respect your man's privacy. You don't have to give any details, just nod your head yes — I'm right— or shake your head no — I'm wrong."

I couldn't help it. When Eddie turned to stare at Simone, I did too, and her coppery skin turned a little richer as heat rushed to her cheeks. Then... she gave a *very* subtle nod, and Eddie and I both burst into laughter, shortly followed by Simone.

"*Told you!*" Eddie bellowed, slapping the counter in triumph as I lifted the wine bottle again to fill a glass for Simone.

"None for me," she said, waving her hand.

What? Record-scratch.

"*You* don't want any wine? Why..."

My eyes narrowed, taking in her sheepish grin and the hand clutched protectively over her belly. A sudden tightness gripped my throat, bringing tears to my eyes as her mouth spread into a full-on smile. "*Simone*, oh my God!"

Eddie embraced her first, since he was right beside her. "Yep, *slanging*, just like I said!" I laughed as I rounded the counter to her to pull her into a hug. Before I knew it, we were both crying. Simone and Roman had suffered a miscarriage seven, maybe eight months ago, so I knew this had to mean a lot to them. In their own way, they had both been a mess, but I know Simone was particularly heartbroken. Now, however, she radiated happiness as she relayed the news that she was fifteen, almost sixteen weeks along, and that Roman knew, and was *thrilled* about it.

We talked late into the night, and I had a smile on my face long after they were gone, thinking about Roman and Simone having a baby. I bit back the onset of something akin to jealousy as I went into my bedroom, dumped my laundry hamper, and sat down on the floor to sort the clothes. As I did so, unpleasant thoughts of never settling with someone that could give me a baby of my own filtered into my mind. Silently, I cursed Darren's name. I knew it was only because of *him* that I was in this unshakable melancholy mood. The breakup with him had been the worst in a *long* time.

Though it didn't compare to what happened in France, the whole "*Surprise, I'm engaged, you're dumped!*" thing was a lot harder to shake than I expected. Granted, not even a week had passed since the breakup, but *still*.

I finished sorting the laundry and packed it into my collapsible hamper, grabbed my detergent and dryer sheets, shoved my phone into the pocket of my terry-cloth lounge shorts, and headed out, locking the door behind me. The laundry room for our floor held three washers and three dryers. All three washing machines were occupied when I walked in, but the timers on the front said that there were only a few minutes left in the cycle. I sat down to wait, not realizing that I'd closed my eyes *or* fallen asleep until the clanging of the washing machine door jarred me awake.

When I opened my eyes, Carter was pulling the last of his clothes from the washing machines to transfer to the dryers. He glanced back, smiling when he realized my eyes were open. "Machines are all yours, sleepy head."

"I had a few glasses of wine," I said, for some reason feeling the need to explain my sleepy state as I stood, loading my own laundry into the machines. Carter nodded, closing the last door on the dryer and hitting a few buttons to start the cycle. Instead of leaving, he lingered, watching me as I measured detergent into the machines, started my own loads, then sat down.

"So I heard you and the stuffed shirt broke up," he said, not even giving me time to get all the way into my seat. "What happened?"

I lifted an eyebrow, watching as he ambled toward me with his hands shoved into the pockets of his sweatpants. I took a deep breath, then hunched my shoulders. "I... I got dumped."

"Seriously?" Carter's eyes went wide as he tilted his head, leaning into the metal counter. "*He* broke up with *you*?"

"Yep."

Carter pulled his face into a scowl. "*Wow.* Why?"

I shook my head first, not intending to tell him anything, but then... something in me snapped, and when I opened my mouth, everything came spilling out. "Um... I found out — on Instagram — that he got engaged, so I confronted him on it. He basically told me that *everything* I thought about our relationship was a lie, and then told me not to contact him again."

Carter seemed stunned into silence for a moment before he gave a slight shake of his head. "Oh. That's... that's *heavy*."

As ridiculous as it was, I chuckled. "Yes, it is. And now... I just feel like a fool. How could I not realize that he— " I looked away as my voice broke. "Um... I'm sorry. This is stupid."

I scooted to the end of the chair to stand up, intending to leave before I further embarrassed myself by dissolving into tears, but Carter caught me by the hand, kneeling in front of me.

"Fuck him." He swiped the tears that sprang free from my cheeks with his thumbs, then cupped my face between his hands. "If that's the shit he was doing behind your back, you're not losing anything, Viv. And *you're* damn sure not the fool."

"I am," I countered, shaking my head. "I gave him my heart, and my body, and... I didn't even *matter* to him... " I lowered my chin as I covered my mouth to hold back a sob. I gave up when Carter pulled me against his chest, allowing myself a few moments to openly cry in his arms. "I don't understand how a grown woman can be so horrible at not getting her heart broken."

"Will you chill? Don't say stuff like that."

"It's the truth," I insisted as I sat up, desperately trying to dry my face with the backs of my hands. "It's like I'm... cursed."

Carter scoffed. "You're not *cursed*." He pulled me into

another hug, and I buried my face into his neck, inhaling the clean, spicy scent of his skin. In that moment, I didn't even care about being overly-familiar. It just felt good to be held like this.

When we finally pulled back, our eyes met. Carter's arms were still around me, and we were close enough that I could have kissed him. I *wanted* to kiss him, and from the way he was looking at me, his gaze drifting down to my lips, then back up, I suspected the feeling was mutual. Instead, we just... *stared,* ignoring the buzzing of the washing machine, followed a few moments later by the dryer.

Then, he smiled that bright, full smile that sent heat and moisture rushing between my legs. "You're gonna be fine, Frenchy," Carter said, patting me on the leg as he stood. "Don't let an idiot have you walking around doubting yourself, okay?"

He didn't wait for my answer as he grabbed his basket and pulled his clothes from the dryers. After a quick "see ya later", he was gone, leaving me feeling slightly confused about what — if *anything* — was happening between us. I shook my head, then stood to transfer my own clothes from the washing machines to the dryers Carter had just vacated.

Later that night — or rather, extremely early the next morning — I sat in my living room folding my laundry. Near the end of the pile, an unfamiliar tee shirt peeked out from underneath my freshly washed bed linens. I smiled when I saw the Fresh Cuts logo emblazoned on the front of the formerly dark blue shirt. It hadn't *quite* reached threadbare status, but was definitely well worn, and the logo was peeling and faded.

A glance at the time on the wall told me it was far from

an appropriate time of day to knock on his door to return it. I started to fold it into a neat rectangle to return once the sun had come up, but I paused for a moment. It was crazy, and I knew it, but something compelled me to bring the shirt up to my nose... just for a teeny tiny sniff. But *damn*, it smelled just like Carter. The same fresh, leathery, *masculine* scent of him clung to the clean shirt, and I knew what I was about to do was weird, but I didn't care. I covered my face with it and inhaled, immediately got aroused, then wondered what the hell was wrong with me.

"Less than a week after a breakup, you are sniffing a man's clothes. That is very emotionally healthy, Vivienne," I said aloud. And *then*, it occurred to me that I was talking to myself. Out loud.

Way to go, me!

I yanked Carter's shirt from my face and folded it, sitting it to the side so I wouldn't forget to give it back. When I finally crawled into bed that night, I consoled myself with the fact that I hadn't felt the need to actually put the shirt on.

That would have been creepy.

***

Every time my path crossed with a light-skinned guy, average height, average build, I thought it might be Darren. Slap a pair of glasses on him, and I was ready to run up, curl my fists into balls, and let out every bit of hurt and aggression I'd been dealing with in the two weeks since the breakup. I was at the point where my former ability to just lock my hurt feelings away and leave them ignored would *really* come in handy, but that skill was conspicuously absent this time around, and I had no idea why.

Perhaps I'd outgrown it. Maybe I'd exhausted my "don't really care anymore", and this was my heart's way of telling me, "*I can't take another beat down. Not like this.*" In any case… I was ready to move on, ready to pull myself out of the doldrums and back into… back into being carefree.

With a heavy sigh, I looked at the airtight container of espresso-infused truffles I'd just finished packing. They were a collaboration with Urban Grind, and I'd planned to send one of the employees to deliver them. On a whim, I decided to do it myself. I needed the fresh air.

I pulled my jacket on and grabbed the container, cringing when the first blast of cold air hit my face. Just last week I'd been fine in only a sweater, but today I found myself wishing I'd brought along a scarf.

When I got to UG, I wasn't surprised at all to see Simone perched at the counter with a plate full of pastries, and a mug of what — with the way she said Roman was playing baby safety police — had to be decaf or hot chocolate. I pulled her into a sideways hug as I approached, then sat down beside her before handing the container of truffles to the head barista.

"What is that?" Simone asked, eyeing the box as the other woman took it to the end of counter, using a clean pair of tongs to arrange them on a display case.

"The truffles you designed." I shrugged out of my jacket and draped it over the back of my chair, then stole a piece of cinnamon roll from Simone's plate. I laughed when Simone beckoned for the young lady behind the counter to bring her several pieces of the chocolate. "You don't think you have enough going on already?" I asked, motioning toward the stack of cookies on her plate.

"You don't think you should mind your business?" she lifted an eyebrow as she popped one of the chocolates into her mouth, closing her eyes as she savored the flavor.

"Roman is gonna get you," I teased. "Those have caffeine."

Simone gave me a playful roll of her eyes. "Roman isn't anybody's *boss*."

"You *must* be doing something you know you shouldn't."

Simone's eyes went wide at the sound of Roman's voice as he approached, peering over her shoulder at her plate. I laughed as she shoved another one of the chocolates into her mouth, then pushed the food in front of me. "Viv, I'm telling you, you're gonna be fat as hell if you keep eating like that," she said, her mouth still full of chocolate as she lifted her cheek for Roman to kiss.

"You know you're not fooling anybody, right?" Roman grinned as he kissed her again, reaching down to caress the cute little baby bump Simone had sprouted seemingly overnight.

"I have no idea what you're talking about." She closed her eyes, sighing contentedly as he kissed her yet again, this time on the forehead, with his hand still resting on her belly.

I needed to look away. Not because I was grossed out, or even jealous, but... okay, yeah, it probably was jealousy. I wondered if anyone would ever look at *me* like that, and rub *my* stomach like that while I grew the life we had created? Would someone be willing to smile while they whispered positively *filthy* things to me in public, which— from the euphoric look on Simone's face, and her bottom lip pulled between her teeth — was exactly what was happening in front of me. They weren't doing anything over the top, but their simple, love-filled interaction oozed such intimacy I felt like I was invading their privacy by gawking like a teenager.

A hand brushed across my back, and before I even looked up, the tingle that washed over my skin told me it was Carter.

"Hey," I said, unable to help the smile that came to my face. He returned my greeting with a smile of his own as he headed to the counter to order his coffee, acknowledging Roman and Simone with a friendly nod of his head. I watched him the entire length of his short journey to the end of the counter, until the feeling that *I* was being watched made me return my gaze to Simone and Roman who were looking at me with barely-veiled amusement.

"When did *that* happen?" Roman asked, nodding his head in Carter's direction.

I shook my head, pursing my lips in phony bewilderment. "When did what happen?"

The two exchanged a look, then turned back to me and said "Hey" in unison.

"I have no idea what you're talking about," I shrugged, stuffing my mouth with another bite of cinnamon roll, hoping that they would let it go.

Roman shook his head. "Nah... before Carter started trying to move in on your friend here, *your* name was always in his mouth, but he was avoiding you cause you had a man. Now that you don't, y'all are exchanging long looks and shit."

"So you're saying Carter was talking about me?"

His eyes went wide. "Ah, man, I think I hear one of my employees trying to get my attention."

He was *actually* saved by the approach of Carter, with a covered disposable cup in his hand. This time, he stopped to give proper greetings, a handshake for Roman, a little side hug and a playful belly rub for Simone, and a *lingering* side hug for me.

Even with the warm greetings, something was *off* about Carter. The usual light in his eyes was missing, and every smile, every laugh as he made small talk with the three of us felt slightly forced. Not that I was any kind of expert on Carter, but I knew to expect a certain level of cheerfulness from him, and today, for some reason, it wasn't there.

"Hey," I said, picking up the last of Simone's truffles from the plate. "You wanna try one?"

My heart sank a little when he shook his head, rejecting the small attempt to cheer him up. "I'm sure it's good," he responded, in a tone meant to soothe the rejection. "I'm not that into really sweet candies and stuff like that... remember?"

I nodded, popping the truffle into my mouth as he said his goodbyes and left, without any of his usual teasing. That stuck with me for the rest of the day, and by the time I made it home, just before the sun was starting to set, I was feeling the same level of melancholy that I'd started the day with. When I flipped on the lights in my apartment, the first place my eyes fell was on the plant Simone had given me a few weeks ago.

Shit.

The leaves were drooping pitifully, despite its place in front of the window, and I suspected that my negligence about opening the blinds to let in sunlight was the culprit. I grabbed it, along with a bottle of water from the cabinet and took it up to the roof, hoping to catch the last few rays of sun before it disappeared for the night. Several of the tenants maintained a rooftop co-op garden, and I nearly pumped my fist in triumph when I saw the artificial sunlamps on timers distributed among the plants. Hopefully, they wouldn't mind me adding my little houseplant to the mix.

I opened my bottle of water and emptied it into the planter, sending up a silent prayer that my sickly-looking plant wouldn't die. Simone would *never* let me live it down, even though I explained to her when she gave it to me that *nurturing* was not my thing, at least when it came to plants.

Satisfied that I'd done all I could, I tossed the empty bottle into the recycling bin and turned to leave. Glancing across the roof, I noticed a familiar figure, perched on the edge of a bench in the covered outdoor seating area. He wasn't facing me, but I would have recognized those locs and broad shoulders anywhere. Carter didn't notice — or perhaps, simply didn't acknowledge — me as I approached. He just kept staring out over the neighborhood, bathed in the last red-orange light of the sun. When I was beside him, he finally looked up, and I almost wished he hadn't.

I'd never seen *this* Carter, with tension so obvious in his jaw, shoulders drooping, no laughter in his eyes. In the time I'd known him, I hadn't experienced him so subdued, so... *sad*. It was so unsettling that it broke my heart... just a little. I'm not sure what drove me to sit down beside him, but I did, laying my head on his shoulder. He remained silent as well, but after a few moments, he slipped his arm around my waist, pulling me a little closer.

"You want to talk about it?" I asked quietly, tipping my head up to look at him.

He looked at me, then shook his head. "Not right now."

"Okay." I nodded, giving him a small grin. "You mind if *I* talk?" I asked.

To my relief, he returned my smile, and even chuckled a little. "Go for it, Frenchy."

So, I did. I regaled him with stories my childhood, misadventures in college, trouble I'd very nearly gotten into with Eddie, anything I could to lift his spirits, and maybe even make him laugh again. I'm sure it was cold, but I didn't notice, focusing instead on the warmth I gathered from his body pressed against mine. The sun was long gone, replaced by the moon and stars by the time we finally stood up, stretched our stiff limbs, and went back down to our floor, where we parted ways.

The next morning, my plant — looking drastically better — was in front of my door, with a bright yellow post-it attached to the side.

"You forgot this last night.
And... Thank you.
— Carter"

***

IT WAS LIKE I STEPPED INTO THE TWILIGHT ZONE. Everybody went quiet, all eyes on me as I entered the door of Fresh Cuts. I guess I should have expected it, as a woman walking into a room full of men, but damn. It was...uncomfortable.

Carter, *all* the way at the back of the shop, was barely suppressing a laugh as I finally put one foot in front of the other and began moving forward. I honestly wanted to bolt out the door, back to a place where stranger men weren't staring a hole through my clothes, but Carter caught my eye and inclined his head, beckoning me to where he was. I kept my gaze focused on his, and as soon as I reached him, he ushered me to the back, into his office.

"Well that was interesting," I said, as soon as the door closed behind us. "Am I some sort of... anomaly or something?"

Carter grinned. "Well... yeah, kind of. A beautiful woman walks into a room full of men, they're gonna look."

"Seriously?"

He nodded. "Yeah, seriously. You've never been in a barbershop before?"

I rolled my eyes, smiling as I pointed up at my hair, which was free of my usual messy bun, in a mass of curls that rested on my shoulders and stretched well above the top of my head. "When would I have occasion to visit a barber?"

"That's right," he teased. "I forgot you're on a mission to grow *all* of the hair."

"Shut up," I said, batting his hand away as he reached for one of my curls. "I came because I wanted to give you something, and I was too excited to wait until later." I cringed about admitting that, but he seemed not to notice.

Good.

Grinning, I held up a black and gold box, imprinted with the Guilty Pleasures logo. "You told me that you are not into chocolate, and I take that as both a personal insult and a challenge."

"It definitely wasn't an insult, I—"

"Uh uh uh," I said, wagging a finger at him as I pulled the top from the box. "You will taste this, you will love it, and your mind will be forever changed." I removed a piece and held it in front of him with my eyebrow raised. "Wait... unless you are allergic. Are you allergic to anything?"

"Not that I know of."

"Good. Then, *eat.*"

Shaking his head, he took the chocolate from me and took a bite, and I could almost tell he was preparing to repeat his insistence that chocolate just wasn't his cup of tea. But then, I saw the exact moment the flavors hit his tongue. He eyes went wide, mouth stopped moving, and he gave a slow nod of his head.

"Damn," he said, popping the other half into his mouth. "It's actually... really, really good. What the hell is in this?"

"You're not just saying that?" I asked, chewing on my bottom lip.

He reached for another piece from the box. "Nah, these things are *good*. Tastes like it might get me drunk if I eat too many, but good. Is that what you're trying to do, Frenchy, get me drunk off chocolate so you can take advantage of me?"

"You wish," I teased, holding the box away from him.

Carter's only response was a smile as he switched gears. "So are you gonna tell me what you're feeding me or not?" he asked, easily maneuvering the box away from me.

"Salted caramel and whiskey truffles. You said that you didn't really have a sweet tooth, so I thought that maybe one that wasn't so sweet, with more complex flavors would be more in line with your tastes."

"Whiskey, huh?"

I nodded. "Yes. A 12-year-old Lagavulin, very smoky, very chocolatey on its own. From my personal collection."

"*Oh*, so this is a special recipe just for me?"

The grin on Carter's face made me blush, and I stammered over my words as I replied. "This is a test run of a new item for the shop," I said, trying to cover.

"You're gonna use 12-year-old whiskey from your *personal* collection for the shop?"

Damn. No, I'm definitely not using a two-hundred-dollar bottle of liquor in a recipe for the shop.

"Well, I... um..."

"Yeah, I thought so," Carter said, chuckling. "So... why do I get the special treatment?"

I sat down on the edge of his desk. "I... I guess I just wanted to thank you, for returning my plant this morning."

"I get personalized chocolate for returning the plant?" he asked. He was standing so close that I could feel the heat radiating from his body, and smell the barest hint of cologne from his clothes.

"Well... I may have had another intention... to cheer you up." I looked up at him with a smile, hoping to gloss over how nervous I was about his possible reaction.

He lifted an eyebrow at my response, and I could tell that I'd surprised him a little. "You did that already, Frenchy. Last night?"

I shrugged, then reached up to wipe a bit of the truffles' cocoa powder coating from the corner of his mouth. "I wanted to be sure." I met his eyes for a moment, my hand still touching his face before I looked away, then slid down from the desk. "In any case, I am happy to hear that you enjoyed them. I'm going to let you get back to work. I'll see you around."

"Yeah," he said. He smiled at me, but his eyes were unreadable. "I'll see you around."

chapter
three

Carter

It wasn't rhythmic enough to be sex.

At least, not *good* sex, with somebody who actually knew what the fuck they were doing.

That's what I told myself about the sporadic banging coming from the other side of my bedroom wall — the wall my apartment shared with Vivienne's. For the past thirty minutes, I'd been unsuccessfully trying to get to sleep, but every time I managed to slip away, there it was again, rattling the wall.

It was only eight at night, and a Saturday at that, but I was mentally drained after a conversation with my mom about my little brother's behavior problems. But... I was drained after *every* conversation with my mother. Still, I was done with this day, ready to move on to the next one, and sleep was the fastest path to that.

Finally, a full ten minutes passed with no banging, and I tried again to fall asleep. I cringed when the sound came yet again, shortly followed by a loud scream, then a series of muffled bumps like a bag of potatoes being dropped to the floor. *That* was concerning.

Groaning, I sat up, tossed my discarded notebook onto my bedside table, pulled on sweats and a tee shirt, then found my way to Viv's door. I knocked, waited a few minutes, then knocked again when I didn't receive an answer.

What if she does *have... company?*

I chuckled. I would definitely be doing her a favor if she had *company* that had her screaming like that. She sounded more scared than anything... *Shit.* With that thought in my head, I knocked again, even louder than before, kicking myself that I hadn't exchanged numbers with her yet. But I was trying to be respectful, trying not to overstep, trying not to come off as a creep, when I knew she was fresh off a breakup. I was pulling my cell from my pocket to get her number from Simone when the door finally swung open to reveal Vivienne standing there in hot pink boy short panties... and *my* shirt.

I couldn't even address *that* at the moment, because she was holding her head, and blood was seeping through her fingers as she scowled. Stepping into her apartment, I closed the door behind me, looking around for anybody else inside. "Viv, what happened?" I asked, trying to pull her hand away so I could see her head. "Did somebody—"

"*No,*" she said with a dry laugh, shaking her head as she made her way through the bedroom into the bathroom, with me close behind. "Although being attacked would be much less embarrassing than what *actually* happened." She bent to open the cabinet under the sink, giving me full view of her ass before she stood again, placing a first aid kit on the counter.

I stepped beside her, pulling a clean towel from her shelf. "Hold still," I said, pushing the hair that had escaped her messy ponytail away from her face so I could see her forehead. She flinched when I pressed the towel against the gash that ran from the top of her forehead to the end of her eyebrow. When the bleeding finally stopped, I carefully cleaned it with alcohol, then covered it with one of the over-sized square bandaids in the first aid kit. "How the hell did you do this to yourself?" I asked, washing my hands.

She shook her head, taking her turn at the sink to run a fresh towel under the hot water to clean the residual blood from her face, hands, and hair. "I purchased new art, and I was trying to hang it. The hammer slipped from my hands, and..."

My eyes went wide. "You did this with a *hammer*, Viv? You could have killed yourself!"

"Ah, but I have a handsome neighbor who would have come to my rescue," she joked with a weak smile as she fixed her ponytail.

"I don't know how much I could have done about a hammer sticking out of your forehead."

Vivienne gave a heavy sigh as she returned the first aid kit to its place under the sink. "The hammer didn't do this," she said, pointing to her forehead. "*This* happened when I smacked my head on the ladder when I fell, trying to make sure I did not kill myself with the hammer."

"Ah, so *you're* the sack of potatoes I heard falling."

"Guilty," she chuckled. "Seriously though, thank you for coming to check on me."

"Well, you screamed, so I couldn't exactly ignore it.

Besides, I was *about* to knock on your door anyway and complain about the noise."

Viv cocked her head to the side. "Seriously? It's not even 8p.m."

"I was trying to sleep."

"At eight o'clock?"

"Yes. That's when the noise ordinance kicks in."

"Oh." She lifted an eyebrow, then gave me a mischievous grin. "What were you gonna do to enforce it?" she asked, teasing me in that sexy, musical accent. I scratched my head, resisting the urge to tell her I would gladly spank that pretty little ass of hers if she kept playing, but instead, she kept talking. "Why are you going to bed at eight on a Saturday? Shouldn't you be out trolling for women?"

I shook my head. "Not tonight. Tonight, I want to *sleep*."

"Well," she said, stepping past me into her bedroom. She cringed at the random spatters of blood dotting the floor, the overturned ladder, and the large chunk the hammer had taken out of the glossy hardwood floor. "You will definitely have quiet from me for the rest of the night. My walls will just be artless, because I am terrified to use that hammer over my head again." She gave a heavy sigh, with a look of dejection that made me want to pull her into my arms.

Instead, I patted her on the shoulder. "Hey, how about I finish hanging these for you, while you put some ice on your forehead?"

"You would do that for me?" she asked, turning to me with an excited smile.

"Yeah. I mean, it's not a big deal. Just show me where you want them."

Viv pointed out the places, and I carefully measured and

hung the hooks to hold the paper-covered canvas prints while she cleaned up the floor, then went to the kitchen for ice.

I reached for the first canvas, tearing off the brown paper wrapping. Blood rushed to my groin, making me glad that my back was to Viv, so she couldn't see my body's involuntary reaction when I held the picture up to look at it. I don't know what I was expecting the picture to be, but a topless Viv, covering her breasts with chocolate-covered hands was *not* it.

This woman is trying to kill me, I thought, unable to peel my eyes away as I hung the provocative image on the wall. All five of the canvases I eventually hung featured Viv in tastefully seductive nude poses, covered in various types of chocolate, plus one of her dripping with caramel that I would have paid good money to hang on my own bedroom wall.

"It was extremely messy, and very hard to clean off afterwards," she said, returning to the bedroom with a bag of ice wrapped in a towel, which she placed on her forehead after she climbed into the bed.

"I can imagine." And I did. My mind drifted to an image of her in the shower, bathroom filled with steam while... I probably shouldn't think about that, but damn... it was *Viv*.

"I had a lot of fun though," she called from her reclined position against her pillows. "It was for a feature, in Sugar & Spice magazine. You know the owner, Cameron Taylor? She's Roman's cousin."

I nodded. "Yeah, I've heard him mention it." For the first time, I tore my eyes from her nude body long enough to notice the Sugar & Spice logo in the corner of each canvas, along with a publication date. "So the issue comes out next month?"

"Mmhm."

"I'll be sure to get a copy."

She smirked, but didn't otherwise respond, and I took that opportunity to gather up the discarded paper to take to the trash. When I was done, I looked around, for the first time taking notice of how different Viv's apartment was from mine. The layout was the same, even though I had a bigger corner apartment, with two bedrooms, but while my place was all dark grays and blacks, hers was an unsurprisingly vibrant mixture of purples, oranges, pinks, and white.

Viv was always dressed in a wild assortment of colors and patterns, which she somehow managed to make look incredibly fly. But then again... *everything* about Viv was fly. Still, it surprised me that she chose such colors for her living space, and I started to say something to her about it, but when I returned to her room, her eyes were closed, and the rhythmic rise and fall of her chest told me she was asleep.

No, no, no.

I sat down beside her on the edge of the bed, gently nudging her shoulder to wake her up. When she finally opened her eyes, I couldn't do anything but stare.

Vivienne was just... fucking *gorgeous*, and I wasn't sure why it always caught me off guard. The wild mass of red-tinted curls, soulful brown eyes, full, sensual lips, and creamy caramel skin covering a body of lush curves... wearing *my* tee shirt. She wasn't even *doing* anything and she was sexy.

"Carter?"

Goddamnit.

I briefly closed my eyes, then shifted positions on the bed as my body responded to her half-whispering my name. "Wake up, Frenchy," I said after clearing my throat.

"You hit your head, you probably shouldn't be going to sleep right now." I smiled when she cut her eyes at me, groaning as she sat up. "Besides... we need to talk about *this*." I tugged at the hem of the tee shirt I'd been looking for since that I day ran into her in the laundry room. *Weeks* ago.

"What about it?" she asked, feigning innocence.

"This is mine, you little... how do you say thief in French?"

"Voleur."

"Yeah. *That*." An embarrassed smile played at the corners of her lips, but she avoided my eyes until I caught the bottom of her chin, gently turning her face back to mine. "Tell me why you're wearing my shirt, pirate."

"So I am a pirate now?"

"Your patch needs to be a little lower," I said, motioning toward the bandage on her head, "But you're out here claiming other people's stuff as bounty, so yeah, you're a pirate. Now stop deflecting and answer the question."

She shrugged. "It is comfortable."

"I *know*. That's why it's my favorite shirt."

"Oh," she said, running her hand over the fabric. "I did not know it was your favorite. I will have it clean and back to you tomo—"

"No," I interrupted, grabbing her hand. "You keep it. It looks better on you anyway."

Viv's lips parted for a second, then she blushed, avoiding my gaze again as she bit her lip. "Umm... are you hungry?" she asked, finally looking in my general direction, more over my shoulder than actually *at* me. "We could order a pizza or something... unless you have something to do?"

Let's see... go to sleep alone, or spend time with Viv, who I've been crushing on from a distance for almost a year?

"I could eat."

—

"This fruity shit is all you have?" I asked, frowning at the raspberry-infused concoction Viv placed in my hand when I asked if she had any beer.

She shrugged. "Unless you want *real* liquor, yes. That's the only beer I have." She turned back to her laptop, to finish ordering our dinner using the pizza parlor's online service. I tried my best to ignore the appetizing view of her bare thighs, almost completely exposed in her current state of dress. I'd hoped that she would put on a bigger pair of shorts, maybe a snuggie or something, since we were going to be alone, behind closed doors, for an extended period of time. But, Viv seemed completely comfortable in my shirt and the tiny pair of hot pink panties she was wearing.

I would have thought it was meant to be a seduction, if she weren't acting so completely innocent. There was no "accidental" touching, no thinly-veiled innuendo, so I pushed away thoughts of those supple golden thighs wrapped around my waist, and accepted it as her just being comfortable in her own home, not trying to get me into her bed — which I would *not* have minded.

"Well, while we're waiting on the pizza, I'm gonna run back to my place and grab a few *real* beers, okay?"

With a playful roll of her eyes, Vivienne nodded. "*I* am going to find a few pain relievers to take. My head is pounding."

I left her rummaging in her medicine cabinet and went back to my apartment. I snagged a few beers from the fridge and headed back, stopping when my phone began vibrating in my pocket just before I got to my door.I put the beers down on the table by the door while I pulled out my phone. One glance at the number on the screen tanked my mood.

Groaning, I took a seat on the couch, and just before it was about to stop ringing and send the caller to voicemail, I slid my finger across the screen and answered the phone for my brother, Roderick.

"Carter? Yo, Cutz, you there man? What the fuck is up, bruh?" he said when I didn't immediately speak. Already, I could feel the stress creeping through my temples, settling in my forehead in response to his rambunctious greeting.

"Yeah, Rod. I'm here. What's going on, man?"

"Not shit. Just wanted to holla at you." Even in my annoyance, I grinned. Rod tried to sound "hard" despite the fact that he simply *wasn't.* His voice was deeper than the last time we spoke, but still held a youthful edge, betraying the fact that he was only 18 years old, still a kid. A *smart* kid, who didn't have to do half of the stupid shit he did.

"Cut the bullshit, Rod. What are you about to ask me for?"

He sucked his teeth. "Damn, Cutz, I can't just call to say whassup?"

"That's never been the case before, so quit stalling. I'm in the middle of something."

"Ohhh. She fine, ain't she?"

"*Rod.*"

"Okay, damn. Mom wanted me to see if I could come and stay with you for a while."

"For what?"

Roderick blew out a breath. "Shit, I don't know. Some bull about you being a good influence or something," he mumbled.

I gave a heavy sigh of my own before I answered, knowing I only had one real option anyway. "Rod... I'm not for any of that nonsense you pull up there with mom. If I even get a *hint* that you're up to anything, your ass is—"

"Out of there, I know. So I can come?"

Leaning back into the cushions, I massaged my temples, trying to alleviate the sudden pressure. "Yeah, you can come. When, and for how long?"

"I'll have to call you back next week. Mom has to talk to the judge so I can be approved to leave."

I scowled. "Is that how you avoided having to go to criminal detention? Mom *talked* to the judge?"

"Yeah, how you know?"

I decided not to mention that the judge our mother had *talked* into keeping his ass free, even after Roderick had gotten into yet another fight, was probably the same guy who had decided to put him on probation. I'd spoken with him before, some curly-haired Obama wannabe who claimed he wanted to ease our mother's mind about Rod's trouble-making by putting him in a program that would correct it. More likely — he wanted Roderick off of her mind because he was sleeping with her, and didn't want her son around ruining the mood.

"Don't worry about it," I said, shaking my head. "I'm pretty sure he's gonna let you go. Just call me back with the details."

"ASAP," he replied, and I couldn't help smiling again.

He couldn't even hide the fact that he was excited. "Ai'ight man, I'll holla at you."

"Hey, Rod," I called out, catching him before he hung up. "A few things, little brother."

"I'm listening."

"Leave the bullshit at home, okay? I'm *not* playing with you. You get on my turf and start fucking up, I will kick your ass and send you home. You got me?"

"I got you, Carter. I swear, I'm not gonna get in any trouble."

"Good. And you're getting a job too. You're a grown man, you're not gonna be hanging around on the Xbox eating up all my food."

"Okay, man."

"Seriously."

"*Okay.*"

"Okay. I'll see you soon."

"Ai'ight, bye."

We hung up, and I scrubbed a hand over my face, trying to rid myself of the perpetual strain of dealing with my brother. A glance at the time told me I'd been gone for nearly thirty minutes, and I was sure that Viv was probably wondering where I was.

When I got back to her apartment, I didn't see her at first. The lights were off in the main area, but light spilled from her bedroom, into the hall. I locked her door behind me, then headed that way. Standing at the bedroom door, the first thing I noticed was that she *still* hadn't put on any pants. Her ass was in the air, weaving back and forth as she searched for something seemingly just out of reach behind the bed.

God help me.

"Frenchy," I called out, averting my gaze as she turned around, eyes wide with surprise.

"Carter! I was starting to think you had forgotten about me." She smiled, and then — apparently oblivious to how erotic she looked with my shirt hiked up around her waist, curls flying free from her ponytail again — resumed her quest for whatever had fallen behind the bed. A few seconds later, she popped up, triumphantly brandishing a remote. "What? Why are you looking at me like that?"

My gaze drifted to her bare thighs, and hers followed, her eyes going wide when she realized what I was indicating. "I'm sorry," she said, climbing down from the bed and walking over to her dresser. "Am I making you uncomfortable? I am usually in much less when I'm home, so it didn't even occur to me. And then with the..." she pointed to her forehead, which was still slightly swollen from her fall.

What the fuck are you doing, dude? You want her to cover up that banging ass body, like... for real?

I reached up, massaging the back of my neck. "I mean... I wouldn't say you're making me uncomfortable, more like..."

"Carter, you do not have to explain. It was completely rude of me." She pulled a pair of bottoms from the drawer and pulled them over her legs. A few moments later, she crawled back onto the bed, in a pair of lycra athletic shorts that were *barely* an inch longer than the panties she wore underneath. She repositioned herself on the bed, and flipped open the box of pizza, which I hadn't even noticed was there. I wasn't sure whether it made me feel better or worse to realize that she'd answered the door for the pizza guy in what she was wearing a few moments ago. I decided to just not think too hard about it.

"We're eating in your bed?" I asked, slipping out of my shoes before I sat down on the other side.

"Well... yeah. It's pizza." She said that with narrowed eyes, shaking her head as if that statement made perfect sense, so I decided not to argue about it. We ate in relative silence, which wasn't necessarily awkward, just... different. I was thinking about the phone call from my brother, and Viv had a gash in her forehead. So, between the two of us, I assumed that neither of us was feeling very talkative until Viv nudged me in the side after returning from a trip to the kitchen.

"Are you going to tell me what is going on with you this time?" she asked, opening a tub of ice cream.

"What do you mean?"

"You know what I mean. You left in one mood and came back in completely different one. So... what happened?"

I groaned, then took the final swig from the last beer I'd brought with me. "If I tell you this, you have to tell me about how you got in "trouble". Deal?"

"Deal."

She extended her pinkie to me, and after a moment of hesitation, I hooked mine around it, ignoring the buzz of attraction between us when we touched.

"Okay. So... I got a phone call from my little brother. He wants to come and stay with me."

Viv lifted an eyebrow, waiting on me to continue. When I didn't, she scoffed. "Is that it?" she asked, shoving a spoonful of ice cream into her mouth. "There has to be more to it than that. Do you not want him around?"

"Not exactly," I said with a heavy sigh, taking the liberty of leaning back onto the bed, hands propped behind my head. "Rod has a tendency to get in trouble for stuff that's just honestly... dumb as hell. At first, it wasn't anything criminal, just worrying the shit out of our mom. Then... this mess he pulled last time, getting caught up in a drug dealing ring at his *school*, of all places. The other boys vouched for him when he said he wasn't actually doing anything, so he didn't get arrested. Just kicked out of school... I just can't relate to him, at all."

"Why is that?"

"Just... I don't know, different mentalities, I guess. My parents divorced when I was pretty young, and when I was twelve, I had to go live with my dad. When I was thirteen... my mom had Roderick."

"*Wow*. So you're more than a decade older than him."

"Yeah. And we were raised *completely* different. My mom and his dad were super easy on him, whereas my dad and stepmom did *not* play around with me. They pushed, and pushed, and pushed. I'm not complaining, I'm just saying...*I* never almost went to juvie. I went to a private college, graduated, got my masters, and I pay my own way in life."

Viv nodded, then ate another spoonful of her ice cream. "Right. You're a successful business owner, but I do have to ask... how do your parents feel about you getting a great education, which I know is very expensive, and then... owning a barbershop?"

I looked at her and laughed. "My parents didn't pay for me to go to school, Viv, scholarships did. Everybody isn't like you, Miss Ecoli Normalize Surprise."

"École Normale Supérieure..."

"Right, that's what I said, Very Bougie Academy. The point is, my parents couldn't afford to pay for school, so I had to bust my ass to do it myself. And that's not to imply that *you* didn't, I'm just saying, I didn't have that option. The barbershop is a family thing, passed down to me when my father died a few years ago. He left me a nice amount of money from his insurance policy, and I put half in savings, invested the other half, with good advice from my college friends. The barbershop makes enough that I can pay for my basics to live, and the interest on my investments gives me plenty of room to play. So, I can have a comfortable life, but still keep my father's dream going."

"Mm. A *comfortable* life. Keep your *father's* dream going. What about what *you* want to do? Because... from the way you talk about it, I get the feeling that barbering is not it. What would you be doing if the barbershop did not exist?"

"Building programs. I worked with a tech startup before my dad asked me to take over with the shop."

"So why aren't you doing that now?"

I shrugged. "Because sometimes it's not about what *you* want to do."

"But... perhaps it *should* be. I got lucky — I actually *like* the chocolate business. It makes me very happy. But... I think that my father would not have given me another option anyway, even if I hated it. He probably would not speak to me... but I would have to do what makes me happy."

"I *promised* though. All my life, he had me at the shop with him, teaching me the business... I couldn't turn my back on it like that."

"I get it," she said, patting my knee. "Now, back to your brother... you think he acts out just because he *can*?"

I blew out a breath. "I don't know why he does the stuff he does. *His* dad died when he was really young. I think Rod was maybe ten. Seems like he's been wildin' since then."

Viv positioned herself on her stomach, feet in the air as she faced me. I tried not to let my mind drift to filthy things as she licked her spoon clean, then stared at it thoughtfully before she spoke. "Perhaps... he is seeking attention then."

I scoffed. "My mom gives that knucklehead *plenty* of attention. Too much, probably."

Viv carefully replaced the top on her ice cream, then shook her head. "No. *Male* attention. *Your* attention." I lifted an eyebrow as she pushed herself up on her knees, then sat back on her heels. "You said you are thirteen years older than him, right?" When I nodded, she continued. "Well, since his father passed away, he's probably looking for the same type of attention and guidance he would have received there. He wants to come and stay with you because who better to be a mentor, and get him back on the right track than his cool older brother?"

"Cool?"

She sucked her teeth. "*That* is what you focus on?"

"I'm messing with you. I think you may be right, but we'll see what he does once he gets here."

"Yeah. Question... that day on the roof... ?"

I nodded. "Yeah, that was Roderick related. My mom called to tell me he might get sent to juvie because he'd been fighting. But, obviously, it got worked out. She *always* works it out for him."

Viv's eyebrows nearly touched her hairline as she reached to put her ice cream jar on the counter.

"What is *that* look about?" I asked.

She shook her head. "Nothing."

"Uh-uh, come on now, say what you have to say."

Viv grimaced a little, then gave me a weak smile. "Have you noticed the tone you use, when you speak about your brother? It is like there is maybe... I don't know... some resentment there?"

"Nope. You're not taking me *there*, Dr. Viv. Now... on to *you*. I'm ready to hear about your troublemaking."

"Ah," she said, dropping onto her side, propped on her elbow. "I *did* make a deal, didn't I?" From this vantage point, I could see her belly button, and the tiny silver hoop that adorned it. "Um... the summer that I turned 22 years old, I fell in love with a man that I should not have. Keep in mind, this was what... nine years ago? Social media was not what it is now. There was no *Instagram* where I might stumble upon pictures of him smiling with his wife and children, or fishing with his father-in-law. The internet was not yet such a place that I could easily find out that he was not the age he claimed to be, or that his job title was much different from what he said it was. The paparazzi, however, was definitely a *thing*. We were photographed together, leaving a private party that he did not want to attend, but I threw a *fit* about it and he indulged me.

You see... usually we were never together in public places. The majority of our time was spent... um... in the bedroom. When the pictures came out, there was a big scandal — surrounding *him*, not me. My face was mostly hidden behind the horribly huge sunglasses I wore, and I had the good sense to cover what was not hidden, but he... he is a very distinctive man, so there was no hiding for him."

"How did you not know he was a celebrity?" I asked, resting my chin on my hand.

She held up a finger. "Ah, he was not a celebrity. He is what would be known here as an investment banker, very well known in the business finance world, which *I* was not a part of. He told me he was someone's assistant, always had to be available at the boss's beck and call. So he was not around often enough for me to grow suspicious... just enough to fall in love. Then, there was a big scandal. The night we were at the party, was the night that law enforcement raided his office. They leaked it to the news organizations, who obviously tracked him down, but I was virtually a nobody."

"But... your parents recognized you."

She smiled. "Of course. And they went... berserk. When I told them that the affair had been going on for two years, I honestly thought my mother would pass out. She screamed at me until she was hoarse. My father... would not even speak to me. And then they packed me up and shipped me off."

"Wow."

"Wow is right. I had no idea that he was much, *much* older than me, or that he had a family. But, now that I am older, you want to know what part *really* gets me?"

"What's that?"

Viv pushed her tongue out to wet her lips, but remained silent for several long moments. I could sense her mood shifting right before me. Her suddenly wet eyes were a dead giveaway. She blinked several times, then swiped away a few stray tears before she finally spoke. "I thought... I..." she stopped, gave a dry laugh, then cleared her throat before she continued. "I really thought that he loved me like I loved him. Before I left France, I contacted him. *Begged* him to see me just one more time, because he was not arrested. I just wanted him to tell me... I guess I wanted to hear that at the very least, he loved me. But... that wasn't the case."

"Why do you think that?" I asked, reaching forward to wipe a fresh round of tears from her face.

She laughed, but there was no mirth in her eyes. "He *said* so. Told me I was too young to know anything about love... implied that I was simply a plaything for him. Very similar to Darren, only luckily, Instagram *does* now exist. So, at least I was not yet in love, right?" She chuckled at her own joke, and then shook her head. "So... after being mislead twice, in pretty much the same way, I find it very hard to believe when you are kind enough to try to convince me that I am not a fool. You see... I know better." Vivienne nodded to emphasize her point, then averted her gaze as she tried in vain to stem the flow of tears.

Our eyes met, and the sadness I saw there made me realize that the woman in front of me was *not* the woman I'd assumed Viv to be, based on appearance alone. She wasn't the giver of broken hearts, she was the recipient. And... that shit made my chest hurt.

"Hey," I said handing her a handful of the napkins she'd brought into the room for our dinner. "I'm sorry for making you talk about this. I didn't mean to upset you. I thought you had done some crazy shit like streaking at a tennis match or something."

She laughed at that, a real laugh, then looked up at me with a smile. "It's okay. You showed me yours, it was only fair that I show you mine," she joked. "But... I think it's about time that I go to sleep."

"Is that your way of kicking me out?"

"Yes. It is. And please take the rest of this pizza with you," she said, pushing the box at me as we stood and headed back to the front of her apartment. "I don't want it to be available when I get up at 2am to eat my feelings."

When we reached the door, she turned to me, her expression serious. "Thank you, for coming to check on me. And for hanging my pictures, and having dinner with me."

"Any time, neighbor," I replied, pulling her into a half-hug as I bent to place a kiss against her forehead. I was surprised when she wrapped her arms around my waist and pushed herself closer with a soft sigh against my chest.

Minutes passed before she finally stepped away, her eyes still somber. "Good night," she whispered, in the same sexy half-raspy voice she'd used to say my name before, but now, it held a note of wistfulness that made me want to drop the pizza box, pull her back into my arms, and kiss away the tears that were forming in her eyes again as we stood there in her doorway.

I'd halfway made up my mind to do it, when somewhere in her apartment, her cell phone went off, buzzing loudly against whatever surface it was on, and simultaneously blasting a song by 2 Chainz, declaring that all he wanted for his birthday was a "big booty hoe".

I lifted an eyebrow at Viv and she laughed, shaking her head as she glanced behind her. "That would be Eddie calling. *He* picked that song."

"Sounds about right," I chuckled. "Good night, Frenchy."

She nodded, then closed the door behind me with a resounding click as she went to answer her phone.

chapter
four

Vivienne

I WAS *JAMMING*.

Alone in Guilty Pleasures' commercial grade kitchen with Beyonce blasting through my earbuds and the smell of freshly-cooked caramel in the air, I was in my zone, dancing and singing along as I rolled tray after tray of truffles. It was late, well past the time I would usually still be at the shop, but Simone had called with a frantic bride on the other line, desperate for assistance with the last-minute addition of a gourmet sweets table at her reception.

I had no complaints about it. I was happy to help, thrilled to receive *advance* payment on the hefty invoice, and glad for the word-of-mouth recommendations my shop would undoubtedly receive. Not to mention, at nearly two months post-breakup, Darren barely crossed my mind anymore. My mood was way up, somewhere in the clouds, and lifted even higher when *Blow* started playing in my ears. For those few minutes, I completely abandoned my work, singing the lyrics into my mixing spoon. I was asking some imaginary man to *"gimme that daddy long stroke"*, whipping my hair net covered ponytail and winding my hips in a circle when I turned around to see Carter standing in the doorway to my kitchen, a grin plastered on his face.

"How long have you been standing there?" I asked, still holding the spoon up to my mouth like a microphone.

"Since somewhere around the point that you didn't want anybody *seeing "Vivi" on her knees*," he said, chuckling.

"So, a while then," I said, blushing as I deposited the spoon in the stainless steel sink.

Carter nodded, looking around as he stepped into the kitchen. "Yeah... did you know your front door wasn't locked?"

"No, actually. I'm so used to just locking it when I leave for the day that it slipped my mind."

"You should be careful... I could have been anybody walking in here, and you wouldn't have even known."

I lifted an eyebrow, then feigned a scowl as he approached, standing right in front of me. "Okay, *daddy*," I said, intending it as jab, but by the way his eyebrow lifted, and the wicked little smirk that spread across his face, Carter thought I was flirting with him.

He took a step forward, and I took one back, trapped by the cold, curved metal edge of the counter. "Say that again."

"Say what?" I asked, hoping that I was the only one who could hear the loud staccato beat of my heart.

Carter chuckled, tugging at the decorative ties of my chef's coat. "You *know* what."

I brought my hands up to press into his chest, but made no effort to push him away. It was a long-standing fantasy of mine, me and Carter in this kitchen, and to be perfectly honest, he would get no resistance from me about making it come true. I let my fingers drift over his chest, up to his neck, and into his locs. The beginning of his arousal was pressing into my stomach when he abruptly pulled away, swiping a hand over his face before he turned around, pretending to admire the carefully prepared rows of white chocolate truffles I'd rolled in white sugar, then drizzled with caramel.

Taking a deep breath, I took a moment to calm myself before I approached him, confused about what had just happened. I didn't say anything, just stood there beside him staring at the sweets, wondering what he saw there that was so interesting.

"Can I have one?" he asked, finally breaking the silence between us.

"Um... yeah." I reached across the counter for the sealed container of irregular extras I'd intended to take Simone. He took one, then nodded his approval as he ate.

"What are you getting ready to do now?" Carter turned to me with a smile, no trace of the awkwardness that had been there a moment before.

"I have to pack these to be delivered in the morning," I said, indicating the rows of sweets I'd deemed "perfect" enough to serve at the wedding. "And then clean up the kitchen before I can go. Why?"

He shrugged. "Just curious... wondered if you wanted to grab something to eat."

Like... a date?

"I'd like that, but I need about an hour to finish up here."

"You need some help?"

I shook my head. "You don't have to do that," I said. "I've got it."

"That's not what I asked you." He smiled again, and despite still feeling confused and annoyed about him backing away from me, I smiled back.

"Sure. You can help."

With Carter's assistance, it took less than half the time I'd quoted to get the chocolates put away, and the kitchen back in spotless condition for the next day. I swapped my chef's coat for my leather jacket, replaced my non-slip kitchen shoes with boots, and used the "emergency" brush in my office to tame my hair into a neat bun. Fifteen minutes later, Carter and I were sharing messy food truck tacos in the park, with the street lamps lighting our path.

We stopped at a trash can to throw away our food wrappers and the cardboard cups from our drinks. Then, Carter caught me around the waist, pulling me close as we headed back to our block. It was *this*, right here, that confused the hell out of me. I didn't understand the push and pull, and heaven knows I really shouldn't have entertained it, but I truly *liked* Carter, sexual attraction aside. He had, purposely or not, carved out a place for himself in my heart as a friend — a *real* friend, not just some guy positioning himself for sex, because frankly... he could have had that already. Instead, he was someone who wiped tears from my eyes, and teased me until I laughed, making my troubles the furthest thing from my mind.

He pulled me closer, holding me a little tighter as we approached a group of young men on the sidewalk, a little too loud, a little too rowdy for a Wednesday night. It was second nature for me to tense up, gripping the back of Carter's jacket as we got closer and they spotted us. Too many times, I'd been followed down streets, threatened for not stopping to talk, or scared into completely crossing the street to rid myself of an unwelcome suitor.

"I got you," he said, briefly lowering his mouth to my ear to calm my nerves. "Excuse us fellas," he called. By his tone, there was no mistaking that his words were a directive, not a request. Briefly, I thought they would not move, but Carter kept his head high, his arm tight around my waist, and at the last moment, they stepped aside to create an opening for us on the sidewalk. I expected to feel terrified as we passed between them, but the unmistakable sense of authority that bubbled around Carter in that moment made his arms feel like sanctuary. Strangely — or maybe not — that turned me on.

"So tell me what you do for fun, Carter," I said, in an attempt to pull my mind away from the wetness that had suddenly pooled between my thighs.

He shrugged. "Hell I don't know. Play basketball, go to UG, kick it with my friends... kick it with you."

"So you don't have any "me" time?"

Carter glanced down at me, raising an eyebrow as we turned the corner onto our street. "I don't think I've ever called it *that*, but yeah, I guess."

"And what do you do?"

"What's with the questions, nosy-ass?"

"Are we not friends now? I'm trying to get to know you."

I stopped on the sidewalk to let him open the door to our building, then nudged him in the side when he still hadn't answered by the time we started up the stairs. "*Fine*," he said with an exasperated groan, even though he was smiling. "I watch TV, I build computer programs, I spend a little time on the Xbox... I write."

"You *write*?" I asked, jogging a few stairs ahead of him so I could turn around and block his path. "Like... what, books?"

"No."

"Then what?" He rested his gaze on the ceiling, then shoved his hands in his pockets as he blew out a breath. "Hey... are you *embarrassed*?"

He shook his head. "I'm not embarrassed, this is just... something I don't really talk to people about."

"Oh," I said, my shoulders drooping as I turned to continue up the stairs, my mood deflated over him pushing me away again. "I did not mean to pry. I'm sorry."

"Wait a minute, Frenchy." I felt a tug at my waist, and looked down to see that Carter had hooked a finger in one of my belt loops, halting my ascent to my apartment. "I didn't mean it like *that*, like you were bothering me."

"Your body language said otherwise," I countered, avoiding his eyes as he stood in front of me. He cupped my chin, turning my face up toward his.

"Poetry. I write... poetry."

An involuntary smile spread across my face. "*Really*?"

"Don't do that," he said, grinning as he pulled back.

"Do *what*?" I asked. "Do you think that I am going to tease you?"

"I would tease *you* about it."

"But you are not *me*. What do you write about?" I asked as we made it to our floor. We stopped in front of our apartments as I dug my keys from my purse.

"Experiences, life... people."

I smiled as I pushed my key into the door. "People? Am *I* people? Did you write something about me?"

"... Maybe." Carter took a step closer to me, then lowered his head, pressing his lips against the new bandage that covered the laceration on my forehead. "How's your head. Is this healing okay?"

"It's healing fine. But back to this poem you wrote about me, I would like to... read... it... sometime," I said, my words punctuated by kisses as Carter finally lowered his mouth to mine. He held my face in his hands as I gave up trying to speak, focusing instead on the pleasure derived from his tongue massaging mine, the way he gently dragged my bottom lip between his teeth, then dove in to kiss me again. I moaned against his lips, savoring the cool, sweet flavor of him, courtesy of the handful of mints we'd shared after dinner. This would be bliss, my hands buried in his locs, body pressed against my door while he explored my mouth, if only there weren't so many damned clothes between us.

"*Goddamnit, Frenchy,*" he said under his breath when he finally pulled away. My heart was racing as he shoved his hands in his pockets, giving the distinct impression it was the only way he was keeping his hands off me.

"What is it?" I ran a thumb over my lips, which were still pleasantly tingling from the kiss. "Why... what am I doing wrong here?"

A pained expression crossed his face before he shook his head, then pulled me into an embrace. "You're not doing anything wrong, Viv. I just..." — he gave a weary, heavy sigh — "we should call it a night, okay?"

"Okay," I said, even though I could feel the beginnings of tears pricking at my eyes. "Good night." Without waiting for a response, I went into my apartment, locking the door behind me. I bit the inside of my cheek, denying myself the emotional outlet of tears.

Not now.

I shook my head as I shrugged my jacket off my shoulders and onto the couch, then unzipped my boots and placed them beside the door. In the bathroom, I surveyed myself in the mirror. Cheeks and nose slightly red from the cold. Lips swollen and slightly red from being kissed. Eyes slightly red from holding back tears. I took a deep breath, then brought my gaze to the mirror again, looking myself directly in the eyes.

"He doesn't want you like that, Vivienne. Friends. *Nothing* more."

Now... if only I could make myself believe that.

***

The first thing I heard when I hit the second-floor landing was Carter, laughing. I rolled my eyes. The *second* thing I heard was a female voice, responding in kind. I rolled my eyes *harder*. It wasn't like I was jealous of whoever was falling victim to his charm this time. I was more annoyed that *I* had to witness it. I'd carefully avoided him for the last week, and now I was going to have to see him while he grinned in another woman's face.

Ugh.

I went up the last flight of stairs slowly, pausing halfway when I realized that his female companion sounded familiar... and had an accent. I took the remaining stairs two at a time, freezing in surprise at the sight that greeted me in front of my apartment.

First, there was Carter, looking... *dear God*, gorgeous, in a deep blue button-up and jeans, freshly twisted locs, and his black-framed glasses, which he only wore when his contacts were giving him a headache. I tamped down my involuntary thoughts of concern, reminding myself that I was mad at him for the insane mixed signals he was giving me.

Then... there was Morgan, my mother, who was practically swooning at Carter's feet. She had her back to me, but Carter was facing my direction, and when he saw me there on the stairs, he cut his eyes toward my mother with a subtle tip of his head. I narrowed my eyes, then followed his gaze to the magazine tucked under my mother's arm. My lips parted in a quiet gasp, and he gave a sympathetic shake of his head.

My mother had seen my photo shoot.

"*Maman*," I said, deciding not to prolong the inevitable. My mother turned, beautiful as always, with flawless mahogany skin, and thick black hair falling in soft waves against her shoulders. She reached for me, kissing both of my cheeks before she pulled me into a hug. "What are you doing here?" I asked.

"Well, this was supposed to be a pleasant little surprise visit," she paused, then pulled the magazine from her arm and held it up, "*Mais j'ai vu ces photos provacative*... so, we have other things to talk about. Your father is *not* happy."

No surprise there.

"Young man," my mother continued, turning to Carter. "Have you seen the pictures of my daughter in this magazine?"

Carter swallowed hard, then wet his lips as he scratched absently at his eyebrow. "I... um... yes. Yes ma'am, I have." He looked at me like he wanted me to help, but I shrugged. What was *I* supposed to say?

She glanced between us, smirking before she directed her attention to him once again. "Very seductive, no? Vivienne is a very beautiful girl... but I'm sure a virile young man like yourself has taken notice of that already."

"Yes ma'am."

My mother's eyes lit up in delight as she beamed at Carter. "Such a polite boy. *Vous avez de relations sexuelles avec lui?*" she asked, turning back to me.

"*Mère! Non!*" I exclaimed, glad that he seemed oblivious to the fact that she'd just asked me — *in front of him*— if I was sleeping with him.

"Why not?" She smiled at him, cupping his face in her hands before sliding them down to his collar, which she straightened. "*Il est... magnifique.* You should." Carter shot me the "rescue me please" look again as she ran her hands over his chest, to his arms, groping his biceps before she finally let him go. "It was *very* nice to meet you, Carter."

He cleared his throat. "Nice to meet you too Mrs. Lambert."

"No," she said, with a coy smile. "Call me Morgan, please."

"Yes ma'am," he said, then practically sprinted down the stairs to get away.

"Did you *have* to do that?" I asked my mother, as soon as we were in my apartment, the door closed behind us. "I mean, the whole French *femme fatale* and all?"

She laughed, shaking her head as she removed her coat. "I was just playing with him, Vivi."

"Yeah, and *he* thinks you want to screw him."

"And if I do?"

I lifted an eyebrow. "*Mère*, please, I—"

"*Relax mon trésor*, I'm joking. Come and sit with me."

I sighed, took off my coat, then joined her on the couch, where she had the latest issue of Sugar&Spice magazine open to the page with my feature. Despite knowing I was about to be scolded, I couldn't help smiling at the pictures. They were tastefully done, with all of the important parts covered by hands or arms in each image. Still, they were overtly sexy, and not the way any parent would probably ever want to see their child. *That* made me cringe.

I had not considered my parents at all when I accepted the magazine's offer for a feature story on my little chocolate shop. Sure, it had been great advertisement for my business, but I'd operated under the patently false illusion that it only affected me, forgetting that the Lambert name was tied to a much, much bigger business than Guilty Pleasures. That was not on my mind when I was vamping for the camera, having thick paint — *not* chocolate — poured onto me. I could not, however, deny that it was incredibly fun.

"Your father is not at all pleased. Very, *very* upset. You see, when you told us that you were being featured in a magazine, your father became very excited. He bragged to anyone who would listen, and ordered many copies of the magazine, to distribute throughout the corporate office, to give to his business associates... you see where I'm going with this, no?"

Of course I saw where she was going. My father had proudly gifted copy after copy of risqué images of his only child's naked body for mass consumption. "Not pleased" was an understatement.

"He was so upset that he could not come to see me?"

She shook her head. "You know how the man is, taking things as a personal slight. I did explain to him that you are no longer a little girl. He will get over it, and learn a valuable lesson about bragging in the meantime. You're a grown woman, Vivi. An intelligent, vibrant, *beautiful* woman, and your body is yours, to do with as you please. Would I be correct in assuming that this was the point of such a provocative look?"

I blushed, but did not answer. Instead, I picked up the magazine, flipping through the pictures. "It's not like I'm showing anything that would not be seen at the beach."

"Exactly. Vivi, you do not have to explain to me, I think the pictures are beautiful." She reached forward, patting my hand in a comforting gesture. "Now... back to this neighbor of yours. I asked you a serious question. *Why* aren't you sleeping with that tall, gorgeous man?"

"So *now* you encourage a sexual relationship for me."

My mother pursed her lips, tipping her head to the side in censure. "This, Vivi, is not the same thing as a naive young woman being coaxed into an affair by a man twenty years her senior. A *married* man, with kids the same age as she."

I remained silent as she continued. "I know you will tell me that nothing is wrong, but that is not true. You are feeling unsettled... sexually frustrated, I dare say. It is all over your face."

I wanted to deny it, but I had no doubt in my mind that she actually *could* see sexual frustration, as she claimed. I was one of a *very* select few people who knew she wrote erotic novels under a pen name. "*Mom...*" I said, settling on a generic plea to leave me alone.

"*Vivi,*" she whined, grinning as she teased me. She

reached forward, brushing my hair away from my face. "He likes you, you know? When I asked him if he knew you, the look on his face... that was the look of a man who is smitten."

"Who?" I looked away, feigning ignorance even though I very well knew she was referring to Carter. I wasn't looking at her, but I could feel her skeptical stare, boring into me until I finally returned my gaze to her face. "He does not like me in *that* way," I said, dropping the pretense. "He is a friend, that is all."

Her expression softened, and she scooted closer to me, speaking in a soothing tone. "He is a friend... but you wish that he was more?"

"*No*," I shrugged, but my eyes must have told a different story, because she gave me a sad smile, reaching up to gently stroke my face.

"Ah, my sweet, benevolent Vivi. Always giving your heart to someone who has not asked for it." She gripped my chin, forcing me to hold her gaze as tears sprang to my eyes. "Sweetheart... you *must* learn the art of being guarded. You think I don't know about this last breakup a few months ago? Even on video call, you wear it all over you. I don't know the details, but Vivienne... you must stop giving so much of yourself to men who don't deserve it. I mean, sex is one thing, but *this*," she said, covering my heart with her hand. "Keep it to yourself until you are sure... okay?"

I nodded, but as my tears broke free I shifted into shaking my head. "That's *so* much easier said than done." My mother pulled me into her arms as I sobbed, rocking me the same way she had after each of my teenage breakups, on into my very early twenties.

Even following the fiasco with Thierry, *after* she'd

verbally ripped me to shreds about being so naive, she embraced me, allowing me to drain my emotions on her shoulder. I cried until I was tired, and she had to leave, in order to catch her flight. She had taken a detour to see me, but her trip across the pond was more business than personal, so I bid her goodbye after a few more tears, and many more kisses and hugs.

It wasn't until hours later, when I was just about to leave to see Roman and Simone sing at Urban Grind, that Carter knocked on my door. I was expecting it, but the sight of him at my door tugged on my heart in a way I didn't understand, and didn't want to.

"What is it, Carter?" I leaned against the doorframe with my arms crossed. He masked it quickly, but I caught the sudden stiffening of his posture, and the subtle intake of breath. He was actually *surprised* by my cold reception.

His forehead wrinkled as he spoke. "Um... I was stopping by to see if you were going to UG tonight, but it looks like you are. You look great," he added, with a tentative smile.

"Thanks," I said, glancing down at my clothes as if I'd forgotten what I had on. Dark jeans, knee length boots, and a thick, oversized coral pink sweater. Nothing special. "I guess I'll see you there." I stepped back, intending to close the door, but he caught it, easily overpowering me to keep it open.

"I was hoping we could walk down there together."

"I'd rather not." I kept my lips pressed together in a tight line, picking at imaginary lint on my sweater as if I was bored as I waited for his response.

"Oh." His shoulders visibly slacked as he slowly nodded. "I... I guess I'll see you there."

"Okay."

I stepped away from the door, ignoring the shock on his face as it swung closed. A few seconds later, he knocked again. Rolling my eyes, I pretended not to hear it as I checked my purse for my keys, cell phone, lip gloss, wallet, and gum. Satisfied that I had everything, I pulled the strap over my shoulder and dimmed the lights, then pulled open the door to leave.

"You're still here?" I asked, barely looking at Carter as I locked the door and started for the stairs. He caught me by the hand, tugging to get me to look at him.

"Frenchy, I'm—"

"My name is Vivienne."

"Viv, I'm—"

" — *ienne*."

"What?"

"Viv-*ienne*"

He rubbed the back of his neck, jaw clenched. "Are you serious?"

"Very." It was childish, and I damn well knew it, but Carter deserved every bit of frustration I sent him, with his constant hot and cold behavior. *Perhaps* I could frustrate him as much as he'd frustrated me.

"*Vivienne*," he said, his expression tense. "I'm sorry about the other night. I shouldn't have kissed you. It was crossing a line we shouldn't have crossed, and I don't really have an excuse for it. But I'm sorry."

I shouldn't have kissed you.

His apology was meant to make me feel better, but instead it felt like a knife being driven deeper, although I knew he was right. It *wasn't* a line we needed to cross, not if we were supposed to be friends. It was *that* realization that made me mumble "apology accepted", then turn on my heels to head down the stairs, with Carter trailing behind me.

Outside, I made my way quickly through the cold, trying not to care that Carter wasn't bothering to catch up, although he easily could have. When I made it to Urban Grind, I didn't even look behind me, just searched the crowd until I found Eddie, then took a seat beside him.

I knew it was a mistake, but I let Eddie buy me several drinks. I hadn't told him or Simone about the kiss, but he could tell something was up. By the time it was Roman and Simone's turn on stage for Open Mic, I had a distinct buzz.

Singing along, I fake-happied my way through their disgustingly cute acoustic version of Keri Hilson and Neyo's *Knock You Down*. But, my faking it turned to real, pure joy when Roman pulled Simone and her adorable baby bump back into the spotlight after their performance and dropped to one knee. Before I knew it, two steady streams of tears were dripping down my face, and I sobbed with happiness for my friends while Roman pushed a gorgeous diamond ring on her finger.

The feeling persisted long after they'd left the stage, and my mood was so high that when I felt arms around me on the dance floor, I didn't pull away. I'd been in Carter's arms enough that I recognized his touch and melted into him, confused as always by the unpredictable display of affection, and aroused by it at the same time. When the song ended, he kissed my forehead before he let me go, then disappeared in the crowd. Through the next few acts, my buzz wore off and gave way to melancholy, which I was starting to get used to. I told Eddie I was going home, turned down his offer to walk me, then left, grateful for the cold winter air on my face. Soon, the cold settled into my bones, and I was just beginning to wish that I'd brought my ear muffs when rapid footsteps behind me made me turn around.

Carter.

This time, he caught up, walking in silence beside me until we reached the door of our building, which— as always — he opened for me. Quiet persisted as we climbed the stairs, but I paused at my door, somehow sensing that he had something he wanted to say.

My back was facing him, but I could feel the warmth radiating from him as he approached, stopping just shy of touching me. "Viv... can I at least call you *that*?" he asked, his voice hopeful as he leaned against the wall. Briefly, I inhaled the soothing, familiar scent of his cologne, then gave him a subtle nod.

"I hope we can get back to where we were... I enjoyed kicking it with you. Talking to you."

I lifted my hand to my mouth, biting my thumbnail as I turned to face him. "I did as well, but... the mixed signals, Carter... I do not want to be confused whenever I am around you. So... you have to figure that out. Good night."

He nodded, giving me a brief smile. "Good night."

Back in my apartment, I stripped out of my clothes and climbed into the shower for the third time that day, hoping, *praying* that this time, a little hot water would do the trick of ruining my pity party, forcing me to snap out of it. When I re-entered my bedroom, I was cleaner, more energized, but unfortunately... feeling no less pitiful than when I'd gone in.

The flashing light on my cell phone indicated that I had a message, so I pulled it from the charger and turned on the screen. I was surprised to see Carter's name there. We'd never before used the numbers we exchanged after my near-death experience with the hammer a few weeks before. I lifted my hand to my head, running my fingers along the still-tender scar, remembering how easy it had been to hang out with, and open up to him that night. And *every* night.

Shaking my head, I unlocked the phone and went into my messages. I laughed aloud, for the first time in what felt like ages when I read the one he'd sent.

"So... I meant to tell you... your mom is fine as hell. Tell her I said "what's up". — Carter."

"Mmhmm. She was flirting with you, but you seemed like you were scared."

When my own message was sent, my eyes fell on the time that his message arrived on my phone. Nearly an hour ago.

"Never. I was being respectful because you were standing there. Your mom could get it. — Carter."

"I'll make sure to tell my dad you said so."

"Damn. Forgot about him. — Carter."

"Mmhmm."

"What are you still doing up anyway? It's past midnight... would have thought you'd be asleep. — Carter."

"Nope. I'm a night owl. And anyway, I'm wired. Too many Black Russians at UG tonight."

"Caffeine got you hyped up? — Carter."

"Yep. That and a hot shower."

"Play fair. — Carter."

"What?"

"I need you to play fair. If we're gonna keep things

friendly, you can't be putting thoughts of you in a hot shower in my head. — Carter."

Hmmm.

I lay back on my pillows, staring across the room at the racy images of myself that had gotten me "in trouble" with my father. Even though he was embarrassed... I did not regret it. Taking — and now, looking at — those pictures, I felt sexy, and powerful, and free. Like a woman unburdened by things like feelings, and a heart. I held up my phone, typing out a message that I reconsidered several times before I finally took the irreversible action of hitting "send".

"Sorry. I actually might get up and turn it on again to let the steam build up. Do some naked hot yoga or something to tire myself out. Unless you have any other suggestions for things I could do to burn off energy?"

I sat back again, waiting on his response, which came back almost immediately.

"Go to bed, Frenchy. — Carter."

"Already there. Got in right after my shower, after I oiled down, didn't even bother putting anything on yet. Probably won't. Maybe just appreciate the feeling of the cool sheets on my bare skin."

"GO TO SLEEP. — Carter."

"I told you, I can't. Maybe an orgasm will help. I can do that right here from the bed too, don't even have to get up."

"You're a terrible person. — Carter."

"Are you saying I've been a bad girl? Perhaps a little punishment..."

"**Goddamnit,   Frenchy.   You're   killing   me.   —
Carter.**"

Mission accomplished.

Satisfied that I'd gotten him hot and bothered, I put the
phone back on the charger and ignored it, climbing under
the covers to do exactly what I'd said and let my sheets caress
me to sleep. Only… I'd been so intent on getting under
Carter's skin that I hadn't bargained for what my little game
would do to *me*.

For nearly an hour, I tossed and turned, unable to calm
my mind enough to drift off to sleep. Out of desperation, I
pulled open my nightstand drawer, but the thought of a self-
induced orgasm just made me feel even more wretched.

Finally, at nearly two in the morning, I climbed out of
bed and slipped on panties, a tank top, a hoodie and a pair of
yoga pants. I shoved my cell phone and keys into the pocket
of my hoodie, slipped my feet into my furry moccasins… and
went to knock on Carter's door.

chapter
five

Vivienne

WE BOTH KNEW WHY I WAS THERE.

Because of that, I couldn't understand why Carter was being so... *tender* with me.

When he opened the door to let me in — after the first knock, so I knew he hadn't been asleep either— we both just stood there, not really looking at each other until finally, he cupped my face in his hands and kissed me. It was a deep, frantic, exploratory kiss, with his hands gripping my waist, which told me he wanted me as badly as I wanted him. So... yes, he knew why I was there, knew what I wanted, which is why it was *baffling* to me that now that I was in his bed, in only my tank top and panties after his slow, deliberate removal of my other clothes, he still hadn't touched me anywhere more intimate than my waist.

Yes, he'd kissed me. Devoured me really, with gentle nips of his teeth, slow strokes of his tongue, and passionate caresses of his lips, but the places I ached for him to taste, fondle, and stroke went woefully ignored.

"Carter," I said, whimpering in pleasure as the warm moisture of his tongue made contact just below my ear.

"Yeah?"

I lowered my gaze to meet his. "I don't need all of this. I'm ready... I was... *ready* when I knocked on your door. You don't have to do this."

Carter sat up. "That dude you were with before, Derrick—"

"Darren."

He lifted a hand, brushing it through the air. "Whatever the fuck his name was... I know he wasn't doing a damn thing for you in the bedroom. And... you haven't been with anybody else since you split with him... right?"

"Right...." A fluttery feeling sparked in my belly when he briefly closed his eyes, his shoulders sagging in visible relief. "What makes you think Darren wasn't good in bed? I've never told you anything of the sort."

His face dropped into a smirk. "You didn't have to. *His* corny ass did. Every time I ran into him, he was smug as hell, especially if you were there. Groping you, making sure I saw it... little dumb shit like that. A man who was putting it down right wouldn't be so insecure... but, you were giving me *the eye* when you were with him, so maybe *that's* why he was insecure."

"I was *not*," I said, smacking him on the shoulder.

Carter scowled. "*Whatever,* Frenchy. You know you wanted me to sneak into your bedroom one night and lay the hammer down on you one good time."

I burst into laughter. "*Lay the hammer down?*"

"Hey. I said what I said, okay?" He chuckled, then leaned forward, placing a soft kiss against my lips. "But... seriously though... tell me if I'm right. Was he *really* getting the job done?"

"He did okay."

Yeah, right.

Truthfully, Darren was a pretty selfish lover most of the time, and it wasn't rare for me to have to go into my night-stand drawer to finish the job. I enjoyed his company, and he was good to me — I thought — so I told myself it was something I could live with. His other qualities were supposed to make up for it. But... that was a pitiful little truth I wasn't about to admit out loud.

"He did *okay*." Carter repeated my words, shaking his head. "See? *That's* why yeah, I *do* have to do this. Let me take care of you, okay?"

I nodded, closing my eyes as his lips found that moisture-inducing spot on my neck again. Was it even *possible* to say "no" to a man wanting to "take care" of you in this way? How was I supposed to deny him, when he was kissing his way down to my stomach and then back up to remove my tank top? There was a sharp intake of breath, then a quiet chuckle when my breasts were revealed, and I opened my eyes to his fascinated stare.

"Are you serious, Frenchy?" he whispered, not really wanting an answer as he ran his thumbs over the dainty silver hoops that pierced my nipples. I closed my eyes, arching my back away from the bed when his mouth replaced his thumb. Carter was completely unhurried as he traced my nipple with his tongue, using his teeth to gently tug my piercing. I whimpered, half in pleasure, half in pain as he used his fingers to pull the other. "Open your eyes."

I followed his instruction, watching through half-lidded

eyes as my nipple disappeared into his mouth. Carter glanced up to gauge my reaction and I nodded, half-desperate to feel whatever was next. He suckled, hard, sending hot electricity from my fingertips to my toes, settling into an intense throb between my legs. He did that again, a little more gently this time, then began a slow massage with his tongue. Switching positions, he gave my other breast the same attention, then lifted his hand to stimulate both sides at once.

Pressure mounted in me like a piece of metal being coiled into a spring, tighter, and tighter, until I could barely breath, barely see, barely feel anything, and then... it released, and I came, squirming and arching my back, pushing myself closer to him in an effort to hold on to the heady sensation as long as possible.

I went limp, eyes closed, chest heaving as I tried to catch my breath and make sense of the fact that Carter had given me an orgasm without even taking off my panties. *It has to be the piercings.* It *had* to be. Darren had certainly never given my breasts such detailed attention, and seemed somewhat turned off by the piercings, so it was a completely new sensation. That was all. It had to be.

When I opened my eyes, Carter was hovering over me, his eyes bright with interest as he studied my face. "Why are you staring at me?"

"Because I like watching you come," he replied, his gaze drifting down to my lips just before he lowered himself to kiss me. He pushed his tongue into my mouth, starting a slow, sensual massage against mine before he eased away. "I wanna see you do it again." Carter whispered those words against my lips as his fingers slid into my panties, sending high-voltage pinpricks of energy rushing over my skin.

He didn't immediately push inside of me. Instead, two fingers glided over my slick, swollen flesh while he manipulated his thumb in slow, torturous circles. "Don't close your eyes," he commanded, meeting my gaze as he finally dipped his fingers into me, eliciting a low moan of satisfaction that didn't even seem like it had come from my throat.

Carter brought his mouth to mine, catching my bottom lip between his teeth as he pushed further, with deep, tremble-inducing strokes that had me rolling my hips against his fingers.

"Do you want me to taste you?" I gave him a vigorous nod, not giving a damn if I seemed frantic or eager, because, hell, I *was* frantic and eager. "Uh-uh. Head nod isn't gonna work. I want you to *tell* me."

I blushed, biting my bottom lip as our eyes met. "I want you to taste me."

Carter smirked, still working me with his hand as he bent to place another pleasurably bruising kiss against my collarbone. He pulled back, suckling both breasts before he kissed a trail between them, then lower. His tongue dipped into my belly button, playing briefly with the silver ring that adorned it before he continued.

He sat up on the bed, hooking his thumbs into the waistband of my panties to slide them over my hips, down my legs, then tossed them across the room. He spread my legs wide, lips parted as he stared, apparently intrigued by what he saw. "Keep your eyes open," he said, and then his mouth was on me.

Carter used the entire width of his tongue to give me a slow, broad lick that brought me up on my elbows, angling my head to watch as he pushed his fingers inside of me again, moving them in a "come hither" motion that made me feel lightheaded with arousal. He used his other hand to spread me apart, then put his tongue to work again, weaving, circling, and zigzagging until I was out of breath, and rocketing quickly toward another release. He put his whole mouth on me, lapping and sucking as he made sounds that left no doubt in my mind that he was enjoying this just as much — if not *more*— than I was.

His face was buried between my legs, thighs anchored on his shoulders and pressed against his ears as he growled something that sounded like a compliment on the way I tasted, but the pressure of another orgasm was roaring in my ears, so I couldn't really tell and didn't really care, as long as his mouth stayed on me until I ... *peaked*. And *goddamn*, there it was, splintering me into a billion pieces before I came back together, gripping handfuls of his locs to keep his mouth on me until the feeling passed, and I could safely collapse onto the bed, chest heaving as I tried to catch my breath.

Then Carter was on top of me again, pushing my hair out of my face so he could kiss me, seducing me with my own flavor as he pushed his tongue into my mouth. "Are you on birth control?" he asked, wiping the evidence of my orgasm from his face with my discarded tank top.

I nodded, and he kissed me again before he pulled back, his expression serious. "If it's okay with you... I really just wanna feel *you*, nothing between us. I've got STD results, medical records—"

"Carter, shut up." I buried my hand in his locs, pulling him into another kiss as I slipped my other hand between us, then into his boxers to grip the smooth, velvety hardness of his erection. I kept my gaze locked with his as I pushed his boxers over his hips, then pressed myself upwards so that we were almost touching. He pulled away though, stepping down from the bed to completely remove his boxers, then positioned himself again between my legs.

He paused, lifting an eyebrow in silent communication that there was no turning back now. This was the end of the illusion that we were "friends". I nodded, and he sank between my legs, filling me to the point of *almost* pain, but enough pleasure that it didn't matter, not even a little. Just that quickly, I was high again, taking hit after hit of him with each slow, slick stroke as he moved inside me.

Carter lowered himself so that my breasts were pressed against him, my piercings making little divots in his hard chest as he buried himself in me over and over, deeper and deeper like he was trying to get himself lost. Hell, maybe that was the point, because *I* was certainly stimulated past the point of knowing or caring what happened next, as long as he didn't stop what he was doing.

"*Oh my God,*" I groaned, shivering as he hooked my leg over his shoulder to push further. "Carter…"

"Yeah Beautiful?" he asked, kissing my neck. "You good?"

"Yeah, I'm good."

He looked up, smiling. "It's good?"

"Yes, it's good," I purred, returning his smile.

"Tell me again."

"It's good."

"Again."

"It's *so* good."

I pulled him down by his locs again so we could kiss, melting together as I moved my hands to dig my nails into the deliciously firm flesh of his butt cheeks. Carter was reaching places I didn't even know I *had*, tugging my earlobe between his teeth, his hips grinding into mine, all a carefully orchestrated seduction to make waves of intoxicating heat rush over me as he pushed me closer to yet another climax.

"*Goddamnit, Frenchy*," he muttered into my hair, his breathing ragged as he gripped my butt to pull me closer, drive deeper, and propel me over the cliff into overwhelming pleasure, just before he reached his own release, thrusting into me with enough force that it probably would have hurt if it didn't feel *so damned good.*

Carter rolled to the side so he wouldn't crush me under his weight by collapsing on top of me. Wrapping his arms around me from behind, he pulled me close, brushing aside my hair so he could kiss the back of my neck. I'm not sure if I drifted off to sleep or not, but when I opened my eyes again, the clock on his nightstand told me it was barely ten minutes later, and Carter was hard against my back, nudging my thighs apart with his knees.

"Again?" I groaned, already feeling pleasantly sore.

He grinned, then lay back, pulling me on top of him. "Frenchy... we're just getting started."

***

"They" say that sex changes everything, and I was certainly finding that to be true.

Luckily for me — for now, at least — the shift that it

brought about in my "friendship" with Carter was... refreshing. Now, whenever the undeniable sexual attraction between us bubbled to the surface, instead of pushing me away, he pulled me aside and kissed me until I was out of breath. Or, sometimes if I teased hard enough, and we could find a place private enough, he would slip his fingers inside me, stroking and caressing me into a secret little semi-public orgasm. Then, when we got to one of our apartments that night, we would make good love in whatever way the mood struck us.

It took us all of a week to fall into a routine, and by a week after *that*, we were at it every night, blissfully oblivious to the aches and pains of putting our bodies through such... vigorous work.

And that was just talking about the sex itself, not what happened before and after.

Carter was touchy-feely with me, which was surprising, but something I didn't mind at all. I thrived on it, especially when we were alone, and he would rub my feet until I fell asleep, or want me in his lap while we watched a movie. He did insanely sweet things like feed and talk to me while I spent hours detangling my curls, or rescue my poor tortured plant from my neglectful care. No big, grand gestures, just little things that told me, without him saying so, that whatever we were doing was about more than just sex for him.

But, I *wanted* it to be just about sex. Friends who have sex is ideally what we would be, but there was no ignoring the fact that my heart only felt satiated when he was around. I *knew* I needed to pull back, put some distance between us to cool my raging hormones, but how was I supposed to do that when it was three in the morning, and he was knocking on my door because he couldn't sleep?

"I'm getting right back in the bed, Carter," I told him, yawning as I stepped aside to let him through the door. I closed and locked it behind him, then true to my word, headed into my bedroom with him close behind. I climbed into the bed, then turned to watch him as he pulled his tee shirt over his head and crawled in behind me, pulling the covers over both of us before he reached to turn off the lamp.

When the room was bathed in darkness, Carter slipped his arms around my waist and scooted closer, so that his body was flush with mine. His hardness pressed against me as he covered the back of my neck with lingering, deliberate kisses intended to make me forget that it was three in the morning and I had to be up at seven to be at the shop at eight, and had barely gotten any sleep myself.

"Carter... seriously. Sleep."

"You're telling me I'm not dreaming right now?"

"*Carter.*"

"*Okay*, Frenchy." He kissed my shoulder. "I'm sorry. Sleep, it is."

I rolled my eyes when he slipped his hand under my tee-shirt to cup one of my breasts, but he didn't do anything more than hold it as he nuzzled his face against the back of my neck.

"You smell good," he said taking a deep inhale of the scented coconut oil I'd rubbed on my skin after my shower.

"Do I usually stink?"

I closed my eyes as he chuckled, then placed another kiss at the base of my neck. "No. You always smell good enough to eat... as a matter of fact, I could...but nah, you said you wanted to go to sleep."

"I hope you don't think I'm gonna fall for that," I said, smiling into the dark.

"I know. I'm messing with you."

"Mmhmm. Why couldn't you sleep tonight?"

He didn't respond, instead running a thumb across my nipple in an attempt to distract me. I pushed his hand away and turned to him. The streetlamps filtered yellow strips of light through my not-quite-closed blinds, casting enough of a glow on Carter's face that I could see the fatigue in his eyes, and the weariness etched in the lines of his jaw.

"Tell me what's going on," I whispered, running my hand over the broad plane of his chest, down to the ridges of his abs. He sighed, then moved closer, resting his head on my breasts.

"Rod got in trouble again." His voice was tired, edged with frustration. "*Shoplifting*, of all things. It's like... goddamn, do you not understand that black kids end up getting killed for that shit?"

"I thought he was coming to stay with you anyway? What happened to that?"

He shook his head. "My mom wasn't sure about him being in the city, but now *I'm* insisting. He got lucky again, since the shop owner knows mom and decided not to press charges, but this could have been his last strike. Always over some *dumb* shit." He groaned, then continued. "Anyway, I'm gonna get him up here, make him get a job. He would need a license to work at the shop, but I'll get it figured out. Make him get his GED since he got his silly ass expelled senior year. You know he was set to be valedictorian? And fucked it up!"

I buried my fingers in his locs to massage his scalp, waiting until some of the tension left his body before I said anything. "Well, if he needs to, he can come and work for me. I think that once he gets here, with someone he can look up to, and relate to, he'll be fine, Carter. Really."

"I hope you're right."

Neither of us spoke again as we drifted off to sleep. A few hours later, my alarm went off, and I extricated myself from Carter's arms to get ready to leave. He was still dreaming when I was about to walk out of the door, a deep, restful sleep that I hated to interrupt, because I knew he was emotionally drained from the mess with his brother.

"Carter," I said, gently shaking his shoulder as I leaned over him. He grunted an acknowledgement, but didn't open his eyes. "I'm about to go, okay? There's a spare key in the bottom of the basket under the wine rack in my kitchen... can you lock up when you leave?"

Another grunt, which I took as a yes. I kissed him on the cheek, then turned to head out, stopping when I remembered something else. "Hey," I said, returning to my crouched position beside him. "Are you still coming to look at my inventory system and stuff for me today?" Carter nodded, and I laughed when he grabbed my pillow, pulling it against his chest.

AT GUILTY PLEASURES, I PINNED UP AND COVERED my hair, then put on my chef's coat and got to work making several batches of fudge. One for Roman's daughter, Zahra, to contribute to her school's dessert fundraiser, and the others would be for sale in the shop. I was pouring the molten, freshly-cooked mixture into buttered pans when Eddie walked in.

"Good morning, Candy Lady," he said, kissing my cheek as he gave me a side hug. "I feel like I barely see you anymore." His tone was impassive, expression deadpan as he pulled away, feigning interest in the bowls of chopped nuts on the counter.

"Ohh, here we go." I grinned as I pushed the pans of fudge to the middle of the counter, sprinkling them with handfuls of the different nuts as they cooled. "Am I in trouble?"

He shrugged. "In trouble for wha— *oh*, you mean because you've completely abandoned your friends so you can get dicked down?"

Rolling my eyes, I pulled the pair of disposable rubber gloves from my hands to begin cleaning up my workspace. "Now you and I both know that's not true. I haven't been around *as much*, but we've still hung out at UG, we've still had our weekly wine and cheese date with Simone, and we have a chips and margaritas date coming up. And Eddie... did I not spend two hours last night listening to you cry over the phone because this week's girlfriend dumped you?"

"I wasn't crying, and *I* dumped *her*. But yeah, you did. *Still*... I don't like how fast you and the barber are doing... whatever it is you're doing.

"We're not *doing* anything...." I shot Eddie a look, quieting him when Carter's voice carried from the front of the shop as he spoke to the cashier. A few seconds later, he appeared at the door to the kitchen, bringing with him the barely-constrained sense of arousal I felt whenever he was around.

He spoke to Eddie first, since he was closer to the door, briefly making small talk before he turned to me with a smile. It only took a moment for him to close the distance between us, and he hooked an arm around my waist to embrace me, then lowered his mouth for a kiss. I obliged, feeling the cold bite of metal in my hand as he returned my key.

I shook my head, pressing it back into his palm. "Keep it. In case you can't sleep again."

Carter's lips parted, eyebrows raised before he nodded. "Okay." He cupped my face, biting his lip before he kissed me again, slow and sweet. Behind us, Eddie cleared his throat, and we reluctantly pulled away. "I'll see you later," Carter mumbled in my ear, slipping my key into his pocket before he turned to go to his original destination — my office — to make some programming changes to my electronic inventory system.

When I turned back to Eddie, he had his chin clasped in his hand, eyebrows pulled down in a scowl. "Call me crazy, but *that* didn't look like "not doing anything" to me."

"We're friends."

Eddie sucked his teeth. "Oh, *please*. You and I are friends. *That*," he said, pointing in the direction Carter had gone, "Is your damned *man*."

"Keep your voice down," I hissed, pulling him into the far corner of the kitchen. "It's not like that, seriously. I mean yeah, I enjoy being around him, and the sex is... *phenomenal*, but we really are just friends."

"He didn't look at you like "just a friend", Viv. And was that a key to your place?"

"It's not a big deal."

"It's *such* a big deal." Eddie grabbed my hands, squeezing

them between his as he pulled them up to his mouth to kiss. His eyes were filled with concern as he continued. "Two weeks ago, you were mad at him. Last week, you were sleeping with him. *This* week, you're giving him a key to your place. Are you even thinking about what you're doing?"

No.

I wasn't thinking, I was just feeling, and Carter made me feel *amazing*.

"There's... no pressure," I said aloud as Eddie released my hands. "No expectations, no rules. He listens to me, and kisses me in public, and makes sure that I come first when we make love. He helps me clean, and takes out my trash, makes me laugh, he cooks me pancakes, he... he makes me *happy*, Eddie."

Eddie smiled, but shook his head. "Look, I *like* Carter, I think he's a good dude. I just want you to be careful, Viv. Okay?"

"Okay."

Later that night, I found myself on Carter's couch beside him, wearing nothing but a tee shirt, trying my best to distract him from the TV screen without being obvious. I slid my bare feet into his lap, rolling my eyes when he didn't even miss a beat on the game he was playing. I let out a quiet huff, then pulled my feet back so that I could sit up on my knees.

Pressing my chest against his shoulder, I leaned forward, gently nipping his earlobe with my teeth. He jerked his head away from me, eyes still glued to the screen, but I persisted, slipping my hand into his lap. Despite his seeming lack of interest, his erection came to life and he laughed, finally turning to me.

"Frenchy, would you —" I cut him off, taking advantage of the moment by kissing him, sliding my tongue into his mouth as I pushed my fingers under the waistband of his pants and boxers to stroke him. He dropped the controller to grip me by the hips, pulling me into his lap. Over my shoulder, there was a commotion on the screen, and we both looked to see that a black overlay, along with the words "Game Over!" in bright red had covered the screen. "See what you did?" he asked, smacking me firmly on the butt.

I giggled, then bit my lip as I pulled him free from his pants. "I needed your attention."

Carter closed his eyes, groaning in appreciation as I sank down on him. He gripped my hips, slowly guiding me up and down to set the pace he wanted before pulling my shirt over my head and tossing it to the floor.

"You've got it."

WHEN WE WERE DONE, NEITHER OF US MOVED FOR A while. His fingers grazed my scalp as our heartbeats returned to their normal pace. I tipped my head back for him to kiss me, then buried my face in his neck again, relishing the feeling of him, still erect inside of me.

"Thank goodness for birth control," I said, giggling as he began thrusting upward again. "Or I would be pregnant with about fifteen of your babies by now."

He laughed, keeping me clutched against his chest as he pressed a kiss to the side of my head. "Maybe one day."

Carter didn't seem to notice that I froze, paralyzed by the implication of what he'd said.

You're overthinking it, Viv.

It was probably nothing.

He had to be kidding.

Right?

chapter
six

Carter

THIS ISN'T HOW IT WAS SUPPOSED TO GO. Mentioning the possibility of babies. Knocking on her door at three in the morning to sleep. *Just* to sleep. Accepting a key to her place. *Using* a key to her place, to get into her door because she wasn't at her shop when I knew her usual schedule like the back of my hand, and she hadn't responded to a phone call or text all day.

I mean, not that it was a problem to be worried about her. It was *normal* to be concerned, because she was a friend. But the empty agitation that filled my chest because I hadn't heard from her all day... that was a problem. *That* was a concern. The lightheadedness, the weak knees, the *gratitude* I felt when I walked into her apartment and found her sitting at her kitchen counter, alive, safe, and seemingly healthy?

Big. Fucking. Problem.

I *knew* that. But ... still. When she turned those big brown tear-filled eyes up at me in surprise at my sudden appearance in her apartment, I didn't turn and get the hell out of there like I knew I should have. I dug deeper.

"Frenchy... what's wrong?" I asked, noticing — but not saying anything about — the two huge bouquets of roses on her counter.

She shook her head as I approached. "Nothing. Foolish things, that should not even affect me anymore, but I am silly enough to allow them to do so anyway." She sniffled, then pulled a tissue from a box on the counter to blow her nose. "You probably think I am such a crybaby. Always emotional about something."

"Nah, you're good. I *do* want you to tell me what's wrong though." I sat down at the barstool next to her, and turned so that we were facing each other.

Viv gave a heavy sigh, then nodded her head in the direction of the flowers. "The white ones are from Darren. Because he is a... a *pig*," she spat, her mouth twisted in disgust, "and he saw the spread in Sugar&Spice. The gist of the actual message was that he and his fiancée are no more, and he realized what a mistake he made, especially after he saw the pictures in the magazine."

My pulse raced as I imagined myself shoving those flowers down Darren's throat, but I remained quiet as she continued. "The red ones are from my father. Or rather, from my father's assistant, on his behalf, because he is still upset with me, and so instead of *calling* me today, which would have meant so much to me, I get meaningless flowers, and a meaningless diamond bracelet, and I really want to just flush all of this down the toilet. I would have rather received *nothing* than this reminder that while he is my father, and supposedly loves me... he does not care for me. Not at all."

She dropped her face into her hands, and I had to swallow *very* hard to get past the lump in my throat as I pulled her against my chest to let her sob. "I know *exactly* how you feel, Frenchy. You've just gotta remind yourself it's not about you. It's about *them*."

"Does that actually work?" she asked, tears streaking her face when she looked up.

I shrugged, then gave her a smile. "I tell you what... I'll let you know, okay?" She laughed as I took her face in my hands, kissing the faint line of the scar on her forehead. "Today hasn't been *all* bad, has it?"

"No," she said, shaking her head. "Not *all*. Everybody is out of town, but Roman and Simone gave me a nice big gift certificate to my favorite spa, and Eddie had a case of my favorite wine delivered this morning. So... no, not all bad, but I wish they were here to celebrate my birthday."

"Your birthday?" As soon as the word "birthday" crossed my lips, she blushed, averting her gaze away from me. "Yeah, Frenchy. I see how you treat me, couldn't even tell me about it, I had to find out on the streets," I teased, even though I *did* feel a little slighted that this was the first time she had mentioned it to me.

She gave me a sheepish smile as she hunched her shoulders. "Well... I did not want you to feel like it was something to make a big deal of."

I pointed to the gifts on her counter. "But it *is* a big deal. Your other friends got you presents."

"Right. I did not want you to think you had to do that too, since we are not that kind of friends."

That feeling right then, like a knife through my chest? *Big. Fucking. Problem.*

"Oh," I said, suddenly feeling a little bit dumb as hell about the little box in my jacket pocket. *Not that kind of friends*. I guess I should be glad for that, glad that she wasn't thinking about anything long term, nothing serious. Hell, we weren't even *friends like that*.

"Carter, that did not come out the way it was intended," she said, placing a hand on my knee. "What I mean is that ... us having sex, it has complicated things enough. I did not want to put you in a position where you felt obligated to do something for me. That may be a bit presumptuous, but... I feel like I know you pretty well, and had you known..."

I lifted an eyebrow. "Did you not *want* me to do anything for you? I mean... I look like a terrible friend when you've got wine, and spa days, and flowers, and diamonds up here."

"I hate these flowers, and jewelry means nothing to me."

Cringing, I reached into my pocket and pulled out the box, which I held out to her. "So... this was probably not the best idea then, huh?"

"Carter," she said, her voice suddenly thick with emotion again. "What is this?"

I smiled. "What... you thought I didn't know today was your birthday?" When she didn't respond, I nudged the box into her hands, and she took it, but left it closed. "I asked Eddie a few weeks ago, which was just in time, because I had to order this, and have it rushed to make sure it arrived in time."

"Really?" she asked, her chin trembling.

"Yes, *really*. See... you think it wasn't a big deal for me to know, but I believe in celebrating people on their birthday. I know you said jewelry doesn't mean anything to you, but... why don't you open the box?"

With shaky hands, she did, staring for a long time before

she looked up at me. "Carter... this is *beautiful*," she said, lifting the charm bracelet from the box. The custom bracelet, filled with tiny hand painted ceramic charms in the shapes of truffles and candy bars, and stamped initial charms, and cocoa mugs and gift boxes molded in silver hadn't cost much at all — probably less than any of the other gifts she'd gotten. But the look on her face... *damn*, that pure, overwhelming happiness... it made me wish I had ordered her five of them.

"So you like it?"

She laughed. "*Like* it? Carter... this might be the *best* thing anybody has ever given me. Put it on me." Chuckling, I obliged her request, fastening the bracelet around her wrist. She held it up, smiling before she turned back to me, throwing her arms around my neck to hug me. "Thank you so much for being my friend," she murmured into my ear, her lips brushing against my skin. That sent blood rushing straight to my groin, and she was halfway in my lap, so I knew she could feel it, but she didn't pull away.

Our gazes caught and held, and she raised her mouth for a kiss, which I happily gave. As always, she was sweet, and succulent, and fucking *delicious*. And gorgeous. And not someone I should be kissing like this, not someone I should be involved with like this *at all*. But I couldn't make myself stop, because Viv was irresistible to me, and I'd wanted her for so long, since that day we bumped into each other outside of our apartments.

I wonder if she remembers that?

I was fresh off the court from a game of two-on-two with Roman and a couple of other dudes, Kareem and Davis. It was early summer, so I was sweaty as hell, just ready to get home and into the shower to wash off the funk. I'd always thought it was stupid, the way the doors were configured between my corner apartment and the one beside me, in such a way that you had to stand in front of the other person's door to get into yours. That day, I was *drained*, and a little thing as simple as getting my keys out of my pocket was taking forever.

Then, the other apartment door was flung open, and five feet, seven or eight inches of *bad-as-hell* barreled right into me, dressed in a midriff-baring top that showed off her belly-button ring, and long, flowing skirt that reached to the sandals strapped around her ankle. I was staring, but I didn't feel bad, cause hell, she was too. Slowly, damn near greedily, she raked her eyes over me, then finally brought them up to my face. Creamy, glowing, deep caramel skin, big soulful brown eyes, a fucking *huge* mass of kinky-curly hair — still jet black back then— and what had to be the prettiest face I'd ever seen.

We recognized each other, obviously, cause we worked on the same block, but this was the first time we'd been close like this. *Alone* like this. I'm pretty sure we took that deep, thirsty, "I really wanna see you naked" swallow at the same time. But I didn't make that request, even though I really wanted to, cause only creeps say shit like that to women they only know vaguely, from seeing them around the neighborhood. Instead, I smiled. Asked her if she was okay, since she ran into me pretty hard on her way out the door.

"Why are you outside of my apartment?" she asked, and a glance down at her fingers tightening around the black aerosol attached to her keys told me I was about to get my ass pepper-sprayed without a quick explanation.

I held one hand up in a conciliatory gesture as I pulled

my keys from my pocket, and unlocked my door. "We're neighbors," I said, smiling again in an attempt to ease her anxiety.

She visibly relaxed when I pushed open the door, and finally, she gifted me with a smile. "Forgive me," she said. "*Living* in this neighborhood is new for me, so I may be a little overly cautious. Vivienne Lambert." She held out her hand to shake mine, and I accepted the gesture, grasping her hand a little tighter than intended when warm energy rushed over my skin at her touch. She felt it too, I could tell, because she abruptly pulled her hand back, clutching a handful of her skirt.

"Carter Dixon. And there's no such thing as too cautious for a woman in the city, but this neighborhood is mostly pretty safe. A few troublemakers here and there, but that's the same everywhere you go, right?"

Now that I was no longer in danger of taking a blast of chemicals to the face, I picked up the hint of an accent as she spoke.

"Very true. But, back to this neighbor thing... so *you* are the one who wakes me up every morning at seven, blasting *Good Morning* through my bedroom wall?" Her voice was stern, but her eyes held the promise of the smile playing at the corners of her mouth.

I pushed my hands in my pockets, leaning against the wall between our doors. "You got a problem with Kanye West?"

"*Graduation* Kanye was not so bad," she replied with a wink as I drew my head back in surprise.

"Ohhh, so you're—"

"What's going on here, baby?"

Over her shoulder, some boring looking dude was coming up the stairs, looking between us over his glasses like a nosy dorm parent. Her back was to him, and she grimaced, just slightly, before shooting me what I could only describe as an apologetic smile as he came up behind her, gripping her possessively at the waist.

"I've been downstairs waiting on you for like half an hour," he said in a loud whisper, damn near putting his mouth on her ear even though his eyes were on me.

She turned her head to frown at him. "It has been more like two minutes Darren, don't exaggerate. I am ready, we can go." She put her attention back on me, granting me one last smile. "It was nice to meet you Carter. I will see you around."

Darren tugged at her waist, pulling her toward the stairs. When they were no longer facing me, he snaked his hand down behind her to grope her ass, which he *had* to know I would be checking out. I denied myself the pleasure of laughing at his heavy-handed need to show me that she was *his*.

"See you around, Vivienne," I called behind them, just to make his lame ass squirm.

She paused, pushing herself up on her toes to see my face over the stair rail. "It's Viv. My friends call me Viv."

Now, she was in my arms, my fingers were inside of her, and she was hot, and wet, and willing, and there was no punk assed boyfriend to interrupt, but the difference was... I *knew* her now, and I *knew* Viv was the kind of girl that was dangerous for me, but she tasted *so* goddamned good, and she was *so* gorgeous, *so* smart, *so* compassionate... why the fuck did I think I could be "just" this girl's friend?

"Carter?" she whimpered, sending a fresh round of blood surging to my groin, making me even harder than I thought was humanly possible.

"Yeah?"

"Bedroom."

I smiled at the "o" her lips formed when I pushed deeper, nearly causing her to lose the delicate balance she had on her tip-toes in front of me. "It's your world, birthday girl."

***

"If I didn't know better, I would say you look like a man in love."

Shaking my head, I tore my eyes away from Viv long enough to smile at Simone, who had come to sit beside me at the counter. It was moving day for her, Roman, and his little girl Zahra, into a bigger townhome in a quieter part of our neighborhood. I'd just finished helping Roman bring in the last big piece of furniture, and was taking a much-needed break, which included watching Viv — who was looking her adorably colorful self, in deep teal jeans and a bright orange sweater — hang curtains, fluff pillows, and just be generally domestic.

"It's not like that," I said, even though I couldn't help returning my gaze to where Viv was now quietly, but animatedly discussing something with Eddie. Her curls flew around her face as she gave an emphatic shake of her head in response to something he said, and then she threw her head back and laughed. *That* was a sound I would never get tired of.

Fucking beautiful.

"Mmhmm. You sure?" There was laughter in Simone's voice, and when I glanced at her, it was in her eyes too. "You can't even stop staring at her long enough to have a conversation with me, Carter. You, my friend, are love-struck."

I sucked my teeth. "Stop playing, Simone. We're just friends."

"Mmhmm." Simone's tone dripped with disbelief, and her eyebrow would be touching her hairline if she lifted it any higher.

"Seriously."

Still, Simone didn't say anything, just clasped her hands over her belly.

"It's *not* like that," I insisted, my eye twitching as I forced myself to not look at Viv.

At that, the corner of Simone's mouth tipped up, and a slow smile spread across her face. "Are you trying to convince *me*... or yourself?"

For a moment, I couldn't say anything as I processed her question. Then I groaned, swiping a hand over my face. "I think we both know the answer to that."

"Yep," Simone said, giving me a soothing pat on the shoulder. "You've got it bad, bro. Now what are you gonna do about it? This is so exciting!"

I drew my head back, lifting an eyebrow. "*What* is so exciting?"

"The prospect of you and Viv as a real couple. You two are friggin' adorable together, and you've had a crush on her for *so* long. And *maybe* this will make me forget that you were gonna *use* me to get over her."

I cringed, mentally kicking myself for ever dropping that little tidbit to Simone. She didn't *really* care that my original approaching of her had been pretty shortly after the high, then immediate low of finding out that pretty-ass Vivienne from the chocolate shop was my next door neighbor... but she had a boyfriend. The level of play that Simone had given me was minimal, because she was already involved with Roman, but she joked regularly about being my "rebound" friend.

"Pump your brakes, Simone. Viv and I aren't a couple, not like that."

"But you just admitted you liked her."

"I *do* like her," I said, keeping my voice low. "I like her a lot, but... I'm just not trying to do the relationship thing right now. I'm not even sure what I'm doing with my *life* right now."

"Ah," she smiled. "So you *are* thinking about dropping the barbershop, doing your programming thing?"

"Not dropping it completely... maybe just pulling back. Not sure yet."

"But once you get settled with that... do you think you might... settle down?" Simone propped her elbow on the counter, dropping her chin into her hand.

"Maybe. I don't know. There's... other reasons that it's best to just... keep it casual." I shrugged, then didn't say anything else, hoping that she would take the hint that this was a topic I wanted to leave alone.

She gave me a little nod of her head, letting me know she did, then reached to place her hand over mine. "Okay. But I want you to be careful. Viv is gorgeous, and big-hearted, and smart, and funny... hell, if I wasn't straight, *I'd* want her. She's a really easy person to fall for, Carter, and for what it's worth, I would *love* to see the two of you together. But if that's not what you're trying to do... just be careful."

I didn't know how to tell her that her warning was *just* a little too late, so I simply nodded, then reached up to scratch my eyebrow. "Monie... I know I don't need to tell you this, but, since I know you're friends with Viv too... this stays between us, right?"

"Of *course*, Carter. I won't interfere... too much."

"*Simone!*"

"What? I'm just being honest with you. I will absolutely not tell her anything you've said, because that's between *us*, but if she comes to me about it, I'm going to give her the best advice I can, just like I would with any other friend. Just like I do with you. Right?"

Reluctantly, I nodded. I trusted that Simone would keep her word.

"Oh, and Carter?" she continued, gripping my hand.

"Yeah?"

"If you hurt her... it's gonna be you and me, pregnant belly and all."

"Trust me," I said, chuckling as I draped an arm over her shoulder. "That's the *last* thing I want to do."

Vivienne

"I'll only be gone a week."

That's what I told Carter when I left his apartment to board my transcontinental flight to Europe to visit my parents. It was a trip my mother insisted on, shortly after my birthday, and she swore my father wanted me there too, but I was unconvinced. He never did call to apologize for *not* calling me on my birthday, but he had called to congratulate me on the impressive numbers I'd done for the last quarter at Guilty Pleasures. So... happy birthday to me, I guess.

My mother brought a car to the airport to pick me up, and the first thing she did upon seeing me settle into the seat across from her was break into laughter. "My dear Vivi... if I did not know better, I would think you *enjoyed* upsetting your father. But then again, you *are* very much like me... so I take that back. I *know* you enjoy upsetting him."

"Everything I do does not revolve around him."

That only made her laugh harder. "Vivi... hasn't it always? Martin is your father, of course your actions will reflect him in some way, but mon trésor... when will you stop acting out to get his attention? The piercings, the pictures... you realize it does not endear him to you, no?"

I stared out of the window. "It is not about endearment, it is about *ownership*. My own, no one else's. Besides, he does not know about the piercings... unless you have said something?" I turned to her as she shook her head.

"Of course not. Not until I am *trying* to kill the man. But *this* one, Vivi, you cannot hide."

"I have no desire to." I retorted.

She smiled. "As you shouldn't. It looks good on you. But... darling — and I know you say this is not about your father — you have to understand that your father... he is not capable of giving you what you seek from him."

"I seek nothing from him."

"Love? Acceptance? Validation? None of those things? They are the only reason *I* see for a thirty year old woman to return home with a new hole in her face, but I have been wrong a few times in my life."

I rolled my eyes. "Mère, please."

She laughed the entire way home, to my parents' private house in the Western suburbs of Paris, then wished me luck as I knocked on the door to my father's home office. It wasn't until then that dread really *did* settle over me. When he came to the door, the first place his eyes fell was on the tiny, brand new stud decorating the side of my nose.

It was my birthday gift to myself, something I'd been wanting to do since my early teens. But, not wanting to face the ire of my father, I put it off, opting instead for the piercings that would only be visible to a carefully — or so I liked to think — selected few. He'd always been adamant, no tattoos, no piercings, he couldn't have me walking around looking like a "freak". But I had no desire to do anything extreme, and it was *my* body anyway, so after Carter finished giving me a *very* happy birthday, I'd dragged him along with me down to Eddie's shop. Even though Eddie wasn't there, his artists took very good care of me, and I was happy with the miniscule ball of silver that now dotted my nose.

My father was *not.*

His lip curled up in disgust, but he said nothing, choosing instead to look at me with the same contempt he might give something stuck to the bottom of his shoe.

"Hello, father. It is good to see you," I said, putting on a false cheerfulness to distract from the fact that my heart was pumping with a horrible sort of adrenaline as I braced myself for when he finally started speaking.

He snorted. "I wish that I could say the same, Vivi, but I would rather not have seen that you made the decision to mutilate your face. *Why?*"

"Mutilate? You make it sound as if I have completely

changed my appearance. Besides... what would our Malian ancestors think of you referring to a facial piercing as mutilation?"

"*You* are not in Mali, are you? You are in France, and I expected that you would have the good sense to present yourself in a way that would not embarrass me in front of my colleagues. I see that I was wrong. So... you are dismissed."

And then... he closed the door in my face. My eyes and throat stung, but I held my head high as I swallowed back tears. I would *not* give him the satisfaction.

I went to my room to unpack, and take a nap to help alleviate the disconcerting effects of the six hour time difference. When I woke up, I took a shower and started getting dressed for dinner, but just before I was about to leave my room, my mother knocked on the door.

From the somber look on her face, I immediately knew I'd been disinvited from dinner. I rolled my eyes, shaking my head as she followed me into the room to sit down.

"You *had* to know this would happen, Vivi, right? He has been the same man for thirty years."

I gave a dry laugh as I took a seat at the vanity to dismantle my hair from the neat bun that had taken nearly fifteen minutes to tame. "And I keep hoping he will change, but I suppose that is a fantasy."

"Indeed." She sighed, then turned to watch me through the mirror. "Vivi... I do hope you know your father loves you."

I scoffed. "You remind of this at least five times a week, mère, yet I never see the evidence."

"That is not true, chéri. Your father has made sure that you had nothing but the best."

"Perhaps if he spent less time doing that, I would see the love you insist is there."

My mother grimaced, then came to sit beside me at the vanity. "Sweetheart ... your father... this is going to sound crazy, but I really think he exhausted his emotional ability in pursuit of me. I was a *hard* woman to catch, and I believe I may have driven him a little bit insane. He is not a man who opens up easily, not one who freely gives himself. He is very much the *opposite* of you. So, the two of you clash. You always have. Your father *is* hard on you, he always has been, but... Vivi, I think you take it harder than he actually is. And I also do not think you see how much you push him as well."

"*I* push *him*?"

She nodded. "Yes, sweetheart, you do. You're looking for some kind — *any* — kind of emotional reaction from him, to the point that even his anger gives you *something*."

"Anger is the only thing I ever get."

"He is a businessman, Vivi. Anger is the only emotion he thinks he can publicly show."

Rolling my eyes, I pulled my brush from the vanity and began pulling my hair into two braids. "That is no excuse. And *publicly*? What, I am just the general population to him, not a daughter?"

"It is *because* you are his daughter. He feels he is setting an example of strength, and integrity, and no-nonsense... the type of man he feels would be worthy of his brilliant, beautiful daughter. And those are *his* words about you."

"If you say so. And for the record, the *last* thing I want is an emotionally deficient man who is incapable of showing love."

I winced when she pinched my leg. "This is still my husband, little girl, mind your manners."

"My apologies mère," I said, turning to kiss her cheek. "I just do not understand how *you*, such a bubbly person, married my father who is... very spiky."

She broke into laughter, wrapping her arms around my waist to pull me into a hug. "Ah, he is not, as you say, *spiky* with me, so my bubbles remain intact. He and I have been together for thirty-five years, and he has certainly changed, in some ways good, in some ways bad... as have I. But... he was ridden very hard by his own father. Not a lot of words of endearment, not a lot of hugs. *Pushing* him, constantly challenging him, that is how his father showed love, by making Martin be the best he could be. But... that worked for *Martin*. I have not yet been able to convince him that it does not work for you."

She kissed my forehead, then stood, heading for the door.

"Do you want me to have something sent up for you, or are you going out for dinner?" she asked, with her hand on the doorknob.

I smiled. "Send something up please. I am still tired, no going out for me tonight."

Nodding, my mother gave me another smile, then disappeared out the door. Fifteen minutes later, the butler delivered a small platter of food, and I ate, even though my stomach felt uncomfortable from the fatigue of travel and the emotional toll of the conversations with my mother and father. As soon as I finished eating, I changed into light pajamas. I was asleep before my head hit the pillow.

& —

"Help me understand why such a beautiful girl looks so sad."

I glanced up, drying my face at the sight of a stranger standing over me as I cried. I'd thought that the quiet spot I'd chosen in one of the greenery areas at La Défense would provide some measure of privacy while I wept my heart out, but apparently not.

I'd just left my father's office, so proud for him to know that I was officially done with my undergraduate studies, and he had promptly dashed my excitement by informing me that he would not be moved until I had completed my Master's. So, yet again, my accomplishment was not good enough. It was never good enough. I was never good enough.

But Thierry disagreed. He saw me that day in the park and sat down, smelling like Clive Christian cologne, and so, so handsome. Smooth bronze skin, a tall, powerful body, seductive green eyes, oozing raw sex appeal...My tears dried very quickly as he lifted a hand to my face to wipe my eyes, diverting that moisture to... another place. I spilled my heart out to him, all of frustrations, all of my disappointments, all of my fears, and he soaked it up.

Thierry had a way with words. Not even an hour after he sat down, I was convinced that my father was a buffoon, and I was the smartest, most beautiful girl in Paris. No... the world. Later that same night, he made me believe I was also the sexiest... and I was hooked from there.

***

That was the type of thing that haunted my dreams whenever I came back to Paris. Memories of how incredibly foolish I'd been with Thierry, constant reminders of the disappointment I was to my father. I was only supposed to stay a week, but once I got there, one week turned into two. My father left for a trip, and my mother wanted to shop, and probe me with questions about why I "looked so well-worked", and was pushing me to extend my second week into a month when I decided to put my foot down and go home.

To America.

To... Carter.

It probably wasn't a good thing, but I missed him terribly. We'd texted back and forth, and talked on the phone a few times in my absence, but that was a pitiful substitute for being in his arms. I would deny it in a heartbeat if anybody asked, but in the six weeks that passed between the first time we slept together and the moment I stepped off the plane, back on US soil, I had fallen for Carter, *hard*. I hesitated at even thinking the words "Vivienne, you're in love", because I truly didn't believe that to be the case.

There was, however, no doubt in my mind that given time, that statement would be true.

And it was terrifying.

I was supposed to be guarding my heart, taking what I needed from a mutually agreed upon arrangement with a friend — *not* falling in love. And yet, here I was, my hand poised to knock on Carter's door and yell "surprise", as if he was sitting around, lovesick and waiting for me to return. How presumptuous of me. I hadn't told him exactly when I was coming back, operating under the assumption that he missed me as much as I missed him. But really, for all I knew, it was business as usual for him, and he was doing whatever

— or *who*ever — he would have been doing if we'd never become "friends". Sure, he'd kept in touch, but Carter had never, on *any* occasion openly expressed romantic feelings for me. Except for when he implied that he'd like me to have his babies someday, which could have been a joke for all I knew. And that beautiful custom bracelet that I wore every opportunity I could. And then... there was the fact that his *actions* were very much those of a man who cared a great deal for me.

Needless to say, I backed away from his door and quietly returned to my *own* apartment, where I unpacked, took a long shower, and then climbed into bed.

But I couldn't sleep.

My mind was racing, battling between a need to pull myself back and un-involve my feelings in the situation with Carter, and a need to satisfy the little voice in my head that was urging me on, insisting that I wasn't imagining recipro-cated feelings. Off in the sidelines, another little voice said "forget all of that... you haven't been with him in *two* weeks! Your body needs some attention!"

Sex won.

Feelings aside, there wasn't even an inkling of doubt about our sexual chemistry, so I climbed out of bed, covered my nude body in the short black silk robe that Carter *loved* to see on me, and went back to his door, hoping that no one else came into the hall. I knocked, drumming my fingers against my leg as I waited for him to answer.

When the door swung open, Carter's mouth slacked, and he stared at me without saying anything until I began to fidget. "Carter, I—"

Carter grabbed me around the waist, pulling me into a

hug that took my breath away. He held me like that for a long time, tight against his chest as he breathed in the scent of my hair. Close like this, I could feel his heart racing, and mine swelled in response.

I gasped when he picked me up, wrapping my legs around his waist as he closed the door then pressed his back into it, staring up at me. Supporting me with one arm, he reached up to push my hair out of my face. "I missed the *hell* out of you, Frenchy."

Tears sprang to my eyes, but didn't fall as I shrugged, then draped my arms over his shoulders, resting my hands at the base of his neck. "It was only two weeks."

"Felt like longer." With his hand still buried in my hair, he kissed me, with a passion that gave the distinct impression he was reclaiming me after my absence. We exchanged very few words as he carried me to his bedroom, deposited me on the bed, then climbed on top of me. He unbelted my robe and then peeled it open, raking his eyes over every inch of my body before they returned to my face.

"What is it?" I asked.

Carter shook his head. "Nothing... just getting reacquainted." He caressed my breasts, running his thumbs over my new jewelry, which created the illusion of dainty silver flowers circling my nipples. Next, he lavished kisses all over me, from the top of my head to my toes, but they were more reverential than erotic. It didn't feel like he was trying to turn me on, more like he was trying to tell me something, and this was the only way.

I gasped when he traded lips for tongue, licking a trail from my ankle to the juncture of my thighs, where he used his thumbs to spread me wider and then settled in, devouring me like he was starved. He stayed there, stroking me with his tongue until I arched away from the bed in release, moaning his name into the cool darkness of the bedroom.

"Did you miss me?" he asked, once he was positioned over me again, balancing himself on his elbows.

I reached up, holding his face between my hands as I kissed him. "Did you have any doubt?"

When we kissed again, it was clumsy, almost frantic, but it only took us a moment to get back in sync. Then he was inside of me, and the weight of him was pleasant against my chest as he drove deep, burying himself as far as he could go. I locked my legs around his waist, whimpering as he began moving inside of me, filling me over and over with a passion that had my thighs quivering in what seemed like no time at all.

Carter turned me over, pulling me onto my elbows and knees and wrapping an arm around my waist to keep me close before he entered me again. He made love to me in strokes that were deliciously, torturously slow, one arm still gripping my waist, the other hand tangled in my hair. "Faster," I begged, and he obliged, filling the room with the sound of our sweat dampened skin slapping together until my arms and legs were so weak with pleasure that I collapsed on the bed.

He pressed on, pinning my wrists above my head with one hand as he drove into me, using the other arm to keep my hips elevated off the bed. I opened my mouth to scream, but I was too choked up with ecstasy to make a sound. I found a burst of energy to rock my hips back against his, meeting him stroke for stroke, feeling the heavy weight of his hardness inside of me while his fingers stroked outside, paired with the exquisite friction of the sheets against my already sensitive nipples pushed me over the edge, and I came with blinding intensity.

I cried out his name, repeating it until he slammed into me one final time and exploded, collapsing on top of me with a ragged breath as I clenched around him. After a moment, he raised up, turned me over to kiss me, then pulled me against his chest.

I closed my eyes. Here, in his arms like this while he drifted in the state of uncertainty between awake and sleep, we felt very *together*. The way he embraced me at the door, the way he'd just made love to me... it seemed silly to doubt that whatever I felt for him was reciprocated. But... hadn't I been under the same mistaken impression with Thierry and Darren? I'd been so certain of their love, so convinced of their devotion that their betrayals — separately, but *especially* when considered together — had knocked me off my feet. Was giving myself so completely again a risk I should ever even deliberate?

No answer for that question came, but the security I felt in Carter's embrace was undeniable. He shifted, burying his face into my hair, and just before he drifted off, pulled me tighter and again murmured the words that brought tears to my eyes and tightness to my chest.

"I *missed* you."

chapter
seven

Vivienne

"OH, SO THAT MOTHERFUCKER HAS *GAME*."

Eddie shook his head, giving me a sympathetic smile before he took another sip from his margarita.

"He's not *playing* me. He wouldn't do that. I don't think he would do that."

I *hope* he wouldn't do that.

Eddie and Simone exchanged glances, but neither said anything in response to my assessment that there was no way Carter would purposely toy with me. "He's not that kind of guy," I said, pushing another bowl of tortilla chips to Simone from across my kitchen counter.

"The kind of single guy that would gladly accept pussy thrown at him from his pretty little neighbor? Girl, please. *Every* guy is that kind of guy."

I rolled my eyes at Eddie and turned to Simone, hoping for a voice of reason. She and Carter were good friends, and I didn't doubt for a second that he'd talked to her about me.

"What?" Simone asked, nearly choking on a mouthful of chips and salsa.

"Tell him that Carter isn't like that. That he wouldn't lead me on."

Simone averted her gaze, reaching to take a long sip from her coke. "Not... intentionally."

My eyes went wide, and I felt like someone had splashed cold water on me. "What the hell does *that* mean, "not intentionally". What do you know?"

"Based on my personal opinion of Carter, I do not believe he would intentionally play with your feelings."

"She's using that word again," Eddie sang, turning his head to pretend he wasn't engaged in the conversation.

I crossed my arms over my stomach. "So... you think he *would* play with my feelings, just not on purpose."

"I didn't *say* that." Simone wiped her hands, then sat back in her barstool. "Why are you sweating this anyway, I thought you said it wasn't serious?"

"It *wasn't*. At least, I didn't think it was until I came back from France, and—"

" — didn't even call anybody to say you were back?"

I sucked my teeth at Eddie's interruption. "*Anyway*, when I got back, it's like things were different. If you had seen the way he looked at me when he saw me at his door, or the emotion when he told me he missed me.... Eddie is saying that it's just game, but I think *Carter* is serious about me. And if he is, that means I can be open about the fact that really... I am too."

Simone lifted an eyebrow. "Open?"

"Yes, open," I nodded. "I don't want to have any doubts, not after my... history. I want us to have a conversation about this, I want to hear him say "Vivienne, I want to be with you.", if that's the case. I want to tell him how *I* feel."

"That's a terrible idea," Eddie and Simone said in unison, heads cocked to the side, eyes wide in alarm. Simone took another sip from her drink before she spoke again. "Look... I'm going to say this to you because I love you like a sister. Carter is not going to respond well to anything that looks like you pushing him toward a commitment."

My shoulders sank. "So... he does *not* feel the same."

"Stop putting words in my mouth, Viv. That's not what I said, at all. I really shouldn't be saying *any* of this to you, because it's not my business, but... Viv, just... go with the flow."

"Go with the flow?" I scowled, brushing my hair back from my face. "With my dating history, you're telling me I should trust going with the flow?"

"I think," Eddie said, draining the last of his margarita, "since *she* is the one who's been privy to how the man feels about you... you should probably listen."

"*I* think you're both crazy if you're telling me I should keep giving myself to this man without knowing his intentions."

Simone raised her hand. "And *I* think that you should let Carter's actions speak for him. Look... I've already said more than I should, but you have to understand... he's not like... like Roman, for example. Roman is very upfront with his feelings, extremely transparent. Carter... is not, but that doesn't mean the emotion isn't there."

"So I should just... what, take your word for it?" I asked, shaking my head.

"I think you *can*. Viv, I totally get it, I understand the hesitation. I would *not* give this advice to anybody else. It is *only* because of what I know about Carter that I even feel comfortable recommending it. Seriously... you say he makes you happy, just keep letting him make you happy. Don't over think it."

"That is easy to say when you are seven months pregnant and have a fiancé who openly expresses his love for you."

Simone scoffed. "The mother of my fiancé's child lived with him for the first ten months we dated. Anybody looking at that would have called me crazy, insisted they were still sleeping together, encouraged me to leave."

"I wouldn't have. I *didn't*, because I know Roman."

"*Exactly.* You didn't warn me off of Roman because you knew the man, and you trusted his intentions with me... do you see where I'm going with this?"

I did, but didn't respond. I was too busy doing exactly what she'd urged me *not* to do: over thinking it. I understood where she was coming from, and I mean... she *would* know. Although the romantic thing didn't work out, she and Carter still talked often. She had insight that I didn't.

While I didn't expect her to divulge the details of their private conversations with me, it would have been beyond helpful for her to give me some of the notes from the margins, or *something*. A clandestine suggestion to "trust the process" did nothing to ease my mind.

When Eddie and Simone realized I was lost in my own thoughts, they continued the conversation without me. Eventually, I joined in again, laughing at Eddie's stories, caressing Simone's belly when the baby moved, but really, my mind was still a million miles away.

***

IL EST MAGNIFIQUE.

That's how my mother described him. *Magnificent*. And really, he was. Sitting in front of the window, with the early morning light glowing on his skin, he was... beautiful. I don't know if Carter would appreciate *that* description or not, but with those gorgeous black locs resting on his shoulders, smooth bronze skin covering his athletically toned body, he looked like ancient royalty.

Magnificent.

Carter was occupied with the chewing of a pen as he stared at the notebook clutched in his hand. He was writing, and had been for at least the last twenty minutes that I'd been awake, watching him alternate between furiously scrawling words on the page and long moments like this, where he would stare off into space as if he were just waiting for the words to appear so he could grab them.

Disturbing him seemed like sacrilege. I was barely even breathing, trying my best to hold on to this moment of quiet between us. Then our eyes met, and a moment of... something else happened. He smiled at me, and his gaze drifted away from my face, but the smile remained as he scanned my nude body. Blushing, I pulled the sheet up to cover myself, and Carter scowled, tossing his pen and notepad onto the desk.

"Come here."

My body moved immediately, not waiting on my thoughts to catch up. *This* is where he had me, moving at his command, completely willing, but still baffled by how I had gotten to this point. He pulled me into his lap, then reclined in the chair. "Why were you covering up? You shy now all of a sudden? Uncomfortable?"

"No," I said, giggling as he peppered kisses over the back of my neck. "I have to start covering up so you don't tire of seeing me naked."

He scoffed. "*Never*. Who gets tired of perfection?"

I sighed as he wrapped his arms around my waist, pulling me back against his chest to nuzzle his face in my hair. "Carter... what are we doing?"

As soon as those words left my mouth, I remembered Simone's warning, not even a week ago, to just let it be, but it was too late now. Carter tensed immediately, pulling away as I turned to face him.

"What do you mean?"

Averting my gaze, I looked out of the window as I answered. "You *know* what I mean, Carter. *This. Us.* What are we doing?"

"Are you asking me if we're in a relationship or something?"

I turned back to him, meeting his eyes, but didn't respond. He scrubbed a hand over his face, tossing his head against the back of the chair. "Frenchy... that's not what we signed up for, you know that."

"I do," I nodded, blinking back the tears that were quickly forming in my eyes. "But... I'm kinda... feeling differently now. I'm... I'm putting my heart on the line here."

He sighed, staring down at the floor as his thumb absently stroked my leg. "I...." He stopped, shaking his head before reluctantly bringing his eyes up to my face.

I swallowed hard, trying not to choke on the painful lump building in my throat. "Just say it."

Carter brought his hand to my face in what seemed like slow motion, caressing my cheek and then burying it in the soft curls at the nape of my neck. "I didn't ask you for your heart."

So there it was.

I didn't ask you for your heart.

My stomach turned into a knot as my chin dropped, and dizziness swept through me as I tried to stand up, stumbling over my own feet. I righted myself quickly, dodging Carter's hands when he tried to grab me. My cheeks burned as I frantically searched the room for the clothes I'd haphazardly discarded the night before, in the midst of what I thought was passion, but now seemed more like straight *lust*.

So, so stupid.

"Viv," Carter said, approaching me as I pulled my shirt over my head, not caring that it was backwards. "I'm sorry, I—"

"No," I held up a hand, smiling with as much forced cheerfulness as I could. "You're right. You didn't." I shook my head, bending to retrieve the panties that were peeking from under the corner of the bed. "It was... unfair of me to burden you with that."

I yanked my panties on, then sidestepped him to retrieve my jeans from the other side of the bed.

"Hold on a second, Viv, can we talk?"

"About what?" I asked, zipping and buttoning the pants. "Unless you're going to tell me...." He dropped his gaze to the floor. "*Right*. You're *not*. So... there's nothing to talk about it. We're fine."

"You're mad at me, we're *not* fine."

"I'm not *mad*, I'm...."

Embarassed? Devastated? Hopeless?

"I just need to go." The tears I was trying so valiantly to

hold back were right on the verge of breaking free, and I knew once they did, it wouldn't be pretty.

"I don't want you to leave, not when you're like this." He tried again to grab my hand, but I stumbled back, clutching my arms.

"Carter, please. I just need a moment. I'm fine."

"I'm looking at you, Viv. You're not. I *know* you're not."

I shrugged. "What do you want me to say to that? What do you think I should do?"

"Let me—"

"Let *you*? Let you *what*? Let you explain why you don't share the same delusion that I had about us? Let you hold me? Comfort me? Make love—" I stopped, biting the inside of my cheek in a last ditch effort to not dissolve into a puddle of tears. "Carter... I'm gonna go."

When he didn't say anything, I hurried past him and into the living room to shove my feet into my shoes, grab my purse, and get the hell out of there. I stumbled into my apartment, my legs weak and wobbly as if I were drunk. Stripping myself of my clothes, I got into the shower and just sat there, letting the water pour over me until it ran cold. I didn't even bother drying my hair, just crawled into the bed and lay there, hoping that at some point the hurt would stop.

And... it did.

Or at least, it lessened, as I tossed the last three months around in my head. This was my own fault, for going right from the break up with Darren into indulging my crush with Carter. He was right. He hadn't asked me for my heart. He hadn't asked me for *anything*. It wasn't his fault that I took a seed and ran with it, creating an illusion of a mutual affection that simply wasn't there.

Late that night, laying in the same place I fell after my shower, hunger stirred, and I realized I hadn't eaten all day. I got up, pulling open the drawer that contained my lounge clothes — now full of *his* tee shirts. I bypassed them all, opting for one of my own.

I was halfway through a bowl of cereal when the rattling of my doorknob sent prickles of fear over my skin. My hand was wrapping around the biggest knife in my block when Carter's face appeared in my doorway, and I remembered that he had a key.

He stepped in, closing the door behind him, and for a long time, neither of us said anything. Then finally, unable to handle the silence, I asked "What are you doing here?"

Carter shrugged, his hands stuffed in his pockets as he joined me in the kitchen, stopping a few feet away. "I was worried about you. You haven't returned any calls or texts all day... I knocked a few times, no answer. I... I don't mean to intrude on your space like this, I just needed to see that you were okay.

I nodded, looking down at the swirls of cinnamon and sugar as I stirred the cereal in my bowl.

"And," he continued, taking another step closer, "I feel like shit for hurting you."

I dumped my now-soggy dinner into the sink, turning on the water to rinse it down into the disposal. "Don't. You haven't done anything wrong, Carter."

"So you *say*."

"*Really*. We're okay."

To prove it, I didn't even flinch when he pulled me into a hug, clutching me against his chest in a way that reminded me of my return from France. Tears pricked my eyes, and we pulled away. I dodged the kiss that he aimed at my mouth, angling my head so that it landed on my cheek.

I shook my head, and he gave me a dry smile in return before he pushed out a deep breath, reaching up to massage the back of his neck. "So... do you want me to leave?"

No.

"Yes."

He gave a brief nod, then kissed me on the forehead and left, without a backward glance. I refused to puzzle over that. Carter didn't get to be perpetrator and comforter at once. I turned off my lights, crawled back into bed, and tried my best to go back to sleep, but I kept having the same nightmare, in which I was constantly picking up pieces from a broken heart.

Funny how it's hard to tell dreams from reality sometimes.

***

For a moment Bria's laughter drowned out my music. I punched up the volume, ignoring the happy sound in preference of Jhene Aiko singing my life in *The Worst*. Even though she was my best salesperson, I seriously contemplated firing her when she giggled again, even louder this time. I snatched my earbuds out, then immediately cursed myself for being angry with her. She was young, pretty, and from the sound of it, flirting with a handsome man. She had plenty to be giggly about.

I hated being so... cantankerous, and for the most part I kept it at bay. I saved my right to wallow in my sullen mood for brief periods of alone time. Other than that, especially around people, I faked a cheerful facade, hoping that if I did it long enough, it would filter into my psyche and actually bring me back into the happy Vivienne I was before I just *had* to open my big mouth.

Only a week had passed since my forced epiphany about my relationship — or lack thereof— with Carter, and although I pretended otherwise, it still hurt. As much as it stung, I answered when he called me, responded when he texted, but I carefully avoided his physical presence. He was being cautious with me, trying to hold on to the fragile threads of our friendship. I wanted to meet him halfway, but how do you smile in the face of the person who rejected love when you offered? Using a cell phone, separated by walls, I could pretend. In person... I could not.

But that was no way to live. Bria laughed again, and I pulled off my rubber gloves, tossing them into the trash as I headed to the front to see what was so damn funny.

Bria's pretty face was pulled into a smile, smooth mahogany skin glowing as she flirted with a young man standing at the counter. He was... *no he's not...* yes, he *was*, holding her hands, as he leaned against my display case, saying something that I wasn't quite in earshot to hear.

"Welcome to Guilty Pleasures," I said, clearing my throat. Bria snatched her hands away, shooting me a nervous smile as she remembered that she was *at work* on her off day from her college classes. The young man was slower to react, taking his sweet time to get his weight off my display before he glanced in my direction.

Sweet Jesus.

He looked just like Carter.

The only slight differences were the low, faded haircut

and clean shaven face. Other than that, he could have been Carter's twin. "You must be Roderick," I said, stepping forward with my hand extended. Carter had called me the day before, asking if I was comfortable with doing him a *huge* favor.

The favor?

Hire Roderick, who Roman had already threatened with death after an out-of-the-way comment about Simone, who had hired him first to help with deliveries. So I did. Because Carter was, supposedly, my friend, and that's what you did for friends. Granted favors, even when you were hurting and it was kind of their fault.

"Yeah, I'm Rod. And you must be one of my future girl-friends cause *goddamn*, you fine. Carter didn't tell me all that. He said you were thirty, but that's cool. I'm into cougars."

Did this child just call me a damn cougar?

He rambled on, but I barely heard him, and definitely didn't respond. *Now* I understood why Carter called it a "huge" favor.

chapter
eight

Carter

I FUCKED UP.

In so many ways that I can't even pinpoint which one was the worst.

Befriending her in the first place, when I'd been wanting her since before she moved in... bad.

Kissing her that night? *Very* bad.

Taking the relationship to the sexual point of no return... that was terrible.

Telling her that I never asked her for her heart... fucking catastrophic, and I had no idea how to recover from it. As soon as those words left my mouth, I knew I'd messed up, but she put me on the spot, when I had no idea Viv was even sweating me like that.

In retrospect, I should have noticed. It should have been pretty fucking clear that "hey genius, she's falling for you", but I was too busy trying to convince myself that *I* wasn't falling for *her*, and now I'd done that last thing I wanted to do.

I didn't get her easy smiles anymore. The same ones that

Eddie, Simone, Roman, hell even *Rod* got were out of reach for me, and instead I got the counterfeit copies. I almost think I would have preferred that she just not talk to me at all, but she was *trying*, and even though I could see in her eyes that she was hurt, I couldn't just stay away. In some ways, it was selfish of me, but after spending the last three months building a connection with her... how was I supposed to just let that go? But on the other side of that, I had no idea what it would do to her for me to just withdraw, and not even be the friend I'd originally set out to be.

So... I stuck around. I called, and I texted, and I stopped by, hoping that at some point, it would stop being torture for both of us. At some point, *something* would click, and we'd fall back into the same easy friendship we'd forged before things got... complicated.

That's why I found myself knocking at her door late one night, two weeks after our falling out, without having called first to say I was stopping by. Rod had only been here two days and was already out with a girl. He'd also already eaten everything he could find, so on my way out to feed myself, I passed Viv's door.

And then I went back.

She'd carefully avoided being alone with me for any extended period of time, so I really didn't expect her to take my offer for dinner. Still, I had to try. Maybe we wouldn't ever get back to that blissful place we were before it all fell apart, but we could get our friendship back.

But then she opened the door. She smiled at me... one of her *real* smiles, the ones that hit me like a shot of adrenaline and damn near took my breath away. And she was wearing my shirt. Was this it? Was this the turning point I was waiting on, where stuff like titles didn't matter, and we could just... be?

Viv's smile dropped into a frown, and she leaned into the doorway as she scrutinized my face. "Carter... is everything okay?"

"What?"

"You ... were staring, without saying anything. Did something happen?"

"What? No... no, nothing happened. I'm good."

"Good," she said, the smile returning to her face. "Um... did you want something?"

Where do I start?

"Yeah... actually. I was seeing if you wanted to grab a bite to eat... hang out or something."

Her forehead wrinkled, and she looked away, glancing around her apartment without answering.

"If you don't want to, that's—"

"No." Viv reached out, grabbing my wrist like she thought I was about to back away. "It's not that, it's just... I'm in for the night. I'm working on some new recipes for the shop, and I'm kind of occupied with that. But... you're welcome to join me if you'd like. I don't have a hot meal for you, but I have enough chocolate to give you a belly ache. If you aren't interested though, I won't—"

"I'm down."

She hesitated for a moment, then for the *third* time in less than five minutes, she gifted me with a smile. "Well... come in."

I closed the door behind me, trying not to stare as Viv led me to the kitchen. She was — thankfully— wearing shorts today, but they were short, and clung to her body in a way

that they may as well not have been there at all. But, that
reminded me of the day she hurt her head, which reminded
me of her bent over with her ass in the air, which reminded
me that *now*, I'd been inside her in that position, and that
just wasn't a place where my mind needed to go.

"You might want to take your shirt off."

"Huh?" I asked, with a slight jerk of my head.

She grinned. "Your shirt. You may want to take it off, so
it does not get dirty." She pointed at her own clothes, and I
noticed for the first time that they were covered in random
splatters of chocolate, sugar, and whatever else she was
working with.

I nodded, then pulled my shirt over my head and tossed
it onto her couch across the room. I looked back, half
expecting her to make a filthy comment, but she wasn't even
looking at me. She had busied herself at the stove, stirring
and moving around the different pots before she finally did
glance up.

"Grab a seat," she said, then turned back to the counter,
where she put on a pair of disposable gloves, and continued
buttering candy bar molds. This was something I'd seen her
do plenty of times, but the amount of care she put into it
always made me smile. I pulled a barstool into the kitchen
and sat down, knowing that if I offered to help she would
simply wave me away. I watched her pour a pot of molten
chocolate into the molds, carefully filling them halfway
before painstakingly added a layer of caramel, then covered
them with another layer of chocolate, which she smoothed
to an even surface before she pushed them aside to cool.

"What are you making?"

Viv flinched, almost as if she'd forgotten I was there, then turned around, smoothing the simple black scarf that was keeping her hair back from her face. "A new recipe that I hope to put in the shop. This batch is for taste testing among my friends." She pulled off her gloves, tossing them into the trash before she leaned against the counter and faced me. "Dark chocolate, cinnamon, and ancho and chipotle chilies. Oh, and a vanilla chipotle caramel filling."

"The butter caramel?"

She grinned. "Does any other kind exist?"

"No," I chuckled. "I guess it doesn't."

Inwardly, I smiled about that. How she had taken me from someone who swore he didn't like sweets to keeping a box of the Guilty Pleasures flavor of the week, I had no idea.

"So... have you programmed the latest, greatest innovation in technology yet?" she asked, walking over to the stove to stir one of the pots.

I shrugged. "Still working on the spam database checker."

"Mmm... I take it that the email you set up is still being inundated with offers for hot local sex?"

"Unfortunately."

"Ah," she said, holding up a finger. "That depends on who is offering. You cannot convince me that "horny soccer mom who wants you *now*" is not appealing, Carter."

I laughed, and after a moment passed of trying to maintain her serious expression, Viv did too. And... *damn*, it felt good to laugh with her like this. And it felt good that she was comfortable enough to joke with me again. And it felt *damned* good to know that she was listening when I told her about my programming project, and that she actually remembered.

"I want you to taste this," Viv said, pulling a plastic spoon from the box she kept on her counter for sanitary tasting. She dipped the spoon in the pot that held her caramel, then into the one with the chocolate, holding her hand underneath it to catch any drips as she brought it to me.

"Wait... this isn't the one with the peppers is it?" I asked, when she pulled the spoon from my mouth. "This tastes like..."

She grinned, then took a fresh spoon from the box and dipped it again. "This same flavor combo of the truffle I made for you, only... not in truffle form."

"I knew it was familiar. Still tastes good."

"Does it?" She asked, offering me the spoon again. It took me a second to realize she was standing right between my legs, so close that if I moved any closer, we would be touching. I wanted more than anything to pull her close, but the memory of the look on her face "that" night, like I'd stabbed her right through the heart, made me keep my hands securely tethered to my knees as she slipped the spoon into my mouth.

Then she kissed me.

There was no lead up, no hesitation on her part before her tongue was in my mouth, her arms draped over my shoulders. I didn't give myself time to second-guess it. I gripped her by the hips and pulled her closer, partaking in the sweet taste of *her* blended with the rich flavor of the chocolate.

I didn't want to let her go. We stayed like that, teasing, caressing, savoring each other with kiss after kiss until she finally pulled away, her chest heaving as she tried to catch her breath. I'd pulled that scarf off her head somewhere around the second kiss, and her hair was wild around her face, making her look so sexy with her kiss-swollen lips and creamy caramel thighs on display that I could barely take it.

"Take off your pants."

I swallowed hard, then ran my tongue over my suddenly dry lips as I processed what she said.

"Carter," she said, stepping closer again to grab at the buckle on my belt. "Take these off."

"Why?"

"Because I want you."

Shit.

How many times had a similar combination of those words been the downfall of a man who was trying not to go there with a woman he *really* wanted to go there with? But this was *Viv*. Sweet, gorgeous Viv, who could ask me to do any manner of outlandish shit and I would do it in a heartbeat, especially when she was looking at me like if I didn't start making moves soon, she was gonna take them off *for* me.

So I stood up, and with her hovering barely a foot away, I toed off my shoes, and took off the damn pants. She smiled at me then, a sneaky, provocative little grin that made my hands sweat and my heart race. I watched in awe as she stuck her entire hand in the pot of chocolate then walked over to me, completely disinterested in the mess being made on the floor. With her clean hand, she yanked down my boxers, and the next moment she was stroking me, the warm chocolate dripping through her fingers as she went.

Well… damn.

"Does this feel good?" she asked, pushing the words out in a breathy whisper that somehow made me harder than I already was. I wanted to answer, but then she dropped to her knees in front of me, and my throat went dry. She took me in her mouth, and I barely remembered what the fuck talking *was*, because she was sucking that chocolate off me like her life depended on it.

Fucking beautiful.

That was the thought that played in my head over and over again as I watched her. Yeah, it felt fantastic, but I was watching *her*, tuned in to *her*, and every little moan of pleasure she gave made it better. Every time her eyes found mine, gauging my reactions to adjust her actions accordingly made my heart surge. I buried my hand in her hair, gently guiding her back and forth as her tongue swirled around me, and she sucked harder, and she took me deeper until she pushed me over the edge.

When she stood up, wiping the corners of her mouth, I immediately went for the waistband of her shorts, intending to return the favor, but she pushed me away.

"Shower," she said, pushing her hair back from her face. "So that we can do other things. You have to make sure that all of the chocolate is off."

I lifted an eyebrow. "Oh... yeah. Okay. Do you wanna come with me?"

"I'm going to clean up a bit in here first. I will be there in a minute." I hesitated as she turned to get a towel from the sink, but then she looked up again, rolling her eyes in playful exasperation. "Would you *go*? I swear, I will be there."

I nodded, and went, even though I still felt a twinge of uncertainty. A few minutes later, I felt the shift in the air as the bathroom door opened, followed by the distinct feeling of her presence. Pulling the shower curtain back, I peeked out, watching Viv as she surveyed herself in the mirror. Her shoulders were slumped, and I noticed for the first time the puffiness under her eyes. She closed them as she inhaled deep, then held that breath, and when she finally exhaled, she opened her eyes, and her gaze locked with mine through the mirror.

For a moment, neither of us moved. I was half in, half out of the hot shower spray, wondering what she was doing. Then she blinked, and when she opened her eyes again, she smiled. She was okay. *We* were okay.

When she stepped into the shower with me, she didn't say anything. The tub was small, so we couldn't help bumping elbows as we washed, then took turns rinsing off. Once we were clean, I backed her against the corner, angling her chin up so I could reach her lips, kissing her there before I ventured lower, to her neck, then her collarbone, then sat down on the built-in shower seat and pulled her in front of me to reach her gorgeous breasts.

Today's nipple rings were tiny silver angel wings, a gift I'd given her after seeing her looking at them online. "You like them?" she asked, biting her lip as I traced a circle around them with my tongue.

"I do... were those a gift?" I pulled one nipple into my mouth, suckling as I pushed my fingers into the non-shower-related dampness between her thighs. Her knees buckled, but she righted herself quickly, grinding against my hand as she brought her fingers to her other nipple.

"Yeah," she moaned. "Some guy."

Viv yelped, then giggled when I reached around her to smack her on the behind. "Just some guy, huh?" The water from the shower spray wasn't touching either of us, but the steam created by the hot water kept the air at a comfortable temperature. I grinned as I lifted her leg, pulling her closer to drape it over my shoulder. She was trembling already, and when I put my mouth on her she lurched forward, nearly losing her balance on the wet shower floor. I caught her at the thighs, keeping her close as she clutched handfuls of my locs, still pressing herself into my face, unaware that she'd almost fallen. I laughed a little in my head, then kept going, luxuriating in her uniquely *her* flavor and aroma. I missed this, nearly as much as I missed *her*, and it didn't have shit to do with sexual gratification — not mine, at least.

To be *very* clear, I loved good sex. Who doesn't? But something about *Viv*, when she came... *goddamn*, she was a sight — and sound— to behold. She wasn't a screamer, not even close. Viv orgasmed with her eyes shut tight, in a symphony of soft, sexy sounds, harmonizing breathy moans and low purrs, whimpering my name while her thighs quaked, and her body trembled. Then she opened her eyes, and she looked so euphoric that I wanted to make it happen again. And again. Just like now.

When she went limp in my arms, I shut off the shower and picked her up. I grabbed one of the oversized bath towels I'd teased her about before on the way out of the bathroom, spreading it across the bed before I laid her down. The city lights shining through the window made her skin glow, and I stood back for a moment, just admiring her, flawless, and sweet, and divinely naked.

"Why are you so perfect?" I asked, positioning myself over her on the bed.

She pressed her lips together, grimacing as she averted her gaze to something over my shoulder. "Don't do that."

I narrowed my eyes. "Don't do what?"

"Say those types of things to me." She shook her head, then opened and closed her mouth a few times like she was struggling for the right words. Finally, she brought her gaze back to mine. "Don't tell me things you do not mean."

Frowning, I pushed aside the damp curls that were sticking to her forehead. "I don't say things I don't mean, Viv."

"*Carter*," she pleaded, reaching up to cup my face. "Let's... just make love to me, okay?"

Something about the way she said that made my chest clench. I looked in her eyes, searching for any clue to how she was feeling. Usually, those big browns of hers were open windows right into her psyche, but tonight they were closed and shuttered, leaving me in the dark.

I opened my mouth to say something, but her finger fell over my lips. With the other hand, she reached between us to grab me, then angled her hips up for me to enter. It took every bit of willpower I had not to immediately explode, enveloped in her snug, dewy warmth. Her fingernails dug into my hips, encouraging me to move, so after a moment, I did. I went slowly at first, watching the litany of emotions that played on her face as her body welcomed me, clutching me tight as I pressed in, grudgingly releasing when I pulled back.

Viv's eyes were open, but just barely, lips parted, letting out airy little coos of pleasure like each stroke was taking her breath away. I kissed her, and she eagerly responded, giving her lips and tongue generously as she raked her hands over my shoulders, chest, and back. Then came one of my favorite parts of sex with Viv — I remembered telling her once that it felt like unlocking a new level— when she really came alive, enthusiastically rolling her hips to meet me stroke for stroke. It wasn't until she was fully relaxed, past the initial feeling that she described to me as a pleasurable pain when I first pushed inside that her body really opened up, inviting me deeper.

I was aching to tell her how fucking *beautiful* she looked, eyes wide open now, panting and gasping as her nails bit into my shoulders. Burrowing in as deeply as I could, I lowered myself so that my chest was flush against hers, burying my face into the crook of her neck. I pulled her skin between my lips, nipping her before I soothed each bite with my tongue. Her sweet body gripped me tight every time, and a few moments later, I felt the trembling of her thighs against my hips, warning me that she was about to reach her peak.

When I looked up, tears were streaming down her face, but her head was thrown back in pleasure. With her arm around my neck, she held me close when she came, pressing her face into my shoulder as her body pulsed around me, pulling me over the edge with her. I shifted positions so I wasn't crushing her under my weight, then pushed away the hair that had fallen over her face. Again, I looked at her, waiting for her open her eyes and give me that blissful look, like always.

It never came.

Instead, she kept her eyes shut tight as her body shook with quiet sobs. I held her close, not knowing what to do or say, but I realized *right* then, this wasn't okay. Viv wasn't okay. *We* were definitely, *definitely* not okay.

***

I was stupid for agreeing to this shit.

Dumb as *hell*.

That, and *only* that was perfectly clear to me as I propped my elbow on the dinner table at my father's house, dropping my chin into my hand. Why my mother and stepmother tortured themselves by bothering to be in the same room together, I had no idea. But, Denise — my stepmother — had invited Rod and I to Sunday dinner, and since my mom and wannabe Obama were in town visiting Rod, it only made sense that they were invited as well.

They were arguing, which was nothing new, so I tuned them out, allowing my mind to drift back to a few nights ago, with Viv. She let me hold her until she was done crying, then pretty much immediately shifted back into that fake-happy state that I thought we were past, and sent me home. It wasn't a pleasant memory, not at all, and I couldn't get it out of my head.

Four days had passed since then, and the shift was obvious. Now, Viv wasn't trying anymore. She hadn't returned any calls, hadn't responded to a text, and she definitely wasn't answering when I knocked, so the only thing that made sense from here was to let her have her space. As much as I hated that, hated the thought of just sitting back and watching while she pulled away... what else could I do? I wasn't about to harass her, and I couldn't force her to talk to me. Especially not when what she wanted from me was obvious.

"Carter, I asked you a question."

I scratched my eyebrow, groaning as I looked up at my mother, Angela. Beside her, *No*-bama (Tim) was shoveling food in his mouth like he'd never eaten before.

"Sorry, Mom. What was the question?"

"I was asking if you'd made any more progress with your programming. Technology is such a hot field right now, I'm sure you could launch your own business and do well. Carter has *always* been such a smart boy," she said, smiling proudly as she shifted the direction of her words to Tim.

"Yes, my son has always been brilliant," Denise chimed in.

Here we fucking go.

"His father and I were *so* proud when he decided to channel that into keeping the barbershop open. Such a wonderful young man, with a good sense of loyalty, and family, and clean values. *We* really raised him right." She gave Angela a nasty little self-satisfied grin as she reached for the plate of biscuits in the middle of the table. "He wouldn't abandon his father's dream."

"Yes, Carter's father was a good man," Angela said through clenched teeth, barely holding her composure. "But this is Carter's life. He's always loved tinkering with computers, building games from nothing, figuring out—"

Denise snorted as she interrupted. "Oh, *I* know that. I bought his first computer for him. I'm guessing you know because he told you stories, since you were too busy getting—"

"*Denise!*" I said, shaking my head at her.

Her nostrils were flared when she turned to me, eyebrow raised. "Boy, who are you calling by their first name? I'm your *mother*, I—"

"*I'm* his mother, excuse you," Angela snapped. "You can throw your little jabs, but don't you forget it."

Denise let out an ugly peal of laughter. "*Ha*! You're

worried about *me* forgetting you're his mother? Did *you* forget how he ended up here with me and his father in the first place?"

"*You old, miserable, bitter—*"

"Watch what you say to me in *my* house, I didn't have to invite you here with your little boy toy. I only did it for the sake of my son."

"For *his* sake? Please! I don't know why you *really* invited me, and I *damn* sure don't know why I accepted. I've been putting up with your bullshit for the last *twenty-five* years, and I'm sick of—"

I tuned them out. I'd been listening to them go at it for most of my life, none of this was new.

"Rod," I said, poking him in the side to get his attention as his head swung back and forth between Angela and Denise. "Let's get out of here man, go shoot some hoops."

In the backyard, there was a slab of concrete and a basketball hoop my dad had put in the week after I came to live with him permanently. He didn't seem keen on the fact that I'd choose a pen and notepad or a computer screen and keyboard over a ball of *any* kind, on any day. He blamed it on my mother, and sent me outside for an hour every day to play on that hoop, and eventually, I got pretty good. Good enough to be on my high school team, which balanced out the stuff that would have gotten me teased and labeled as a nerd.

I grabbed the ball from my old room and led Rod outside, grateful for the hoodie I'd worn to shield against the early winter weather. We played in silence for several long minutes before Roderick caught the ball, tossing it between his hands as he spoke.

"So, about Vivienne... dude, she is *bad*."

"Yeah, pass the ball."

He ignored me, throwing it into the air and barely catching it before he continued. "I think I can convince her to let me hit."

I tried to block out the pulsing throb that started at my temple. "*Pass the ball*."

He did this time, and I caught it, dribbling as he kept talking.

"Yo, she's French too? With that sexy ass accent. She's moody as hell, but I bet she's a damn *freak* in the — *ouch*, man! What the fuck was that?" he asked as the ball bounced off his head and rolled away.

My expression was deadpan as I stood up straight, arms crossed in front of me. "Oh no, what happened? Did I accidentally hit you?" I asked dryly, fighting back the urge to laugh at his scowl.

"Accidentally? Dude, you just tried to knock my damn head off my shoulders. You must want her for yourself or something." He pulled his hand away from the slightly raised swelling on his head to look at me. "Or... dude... you're *already* hitting that, aren't you? *Yooo*, respect man." He approached me with his fist raised in front of him, oblivious to the look of death I was giving him.

"Rod, if I lift my fist, it's damn sure not gonna be to give you dap. Change the subject before I kick your ass."

"So sensitive about this chick, *damn*," he said, laughing as he cupped his hand over his mouth. "You caught feelings didn't you? Pussy that good, huh? I'm not surprised, bruh, and that *mouth*. Looks like she could suck the soul out of — Okay man, *shit*!" He said, his voice turning to a higher pitch as he dodged the fist I sent swinging his way and jogged to the other side of the court. "I'm just fucking with you man, I didn't know that was your girl."

"She's not my girl," I snapped. "But that doesn't mean I wanna hear you talking about her like that. How would you feel about Tim talking to some other punk-ass men about our mom like that?"

"But... mom *is* his girl, so I'm not sure I get your— "

I sucked my teeth. "Shut up, dude."

Smirking, Roderick shook his head, then retrieved the ball from where it had rolled onto the grass. He bent his knees then shot, sending it flying smoothly through the goal. "So... speaking of mom... you hardly ever come see her anymore," he said, not looking at me as he caught his own rebound, then sent the ball through the net again.

It didn't take much for me to read the unspoken meaning behind his words, his *real* complaint. I hadn't been to see my mom, which meant I hadn't been to see *him* either.

"Just... busy I guess. I don't know." I shrugged, shoving my hands into the pocket of my hoodie as I watched him run through shooting drills.

His expression was scornful, face coated with a light sheen of sweat when he paused to turn to me. "Liar."

I ran my tongue over my teeth, but didn't respond to his accusation. It was accurate... what was I supposed to say?

"So how *did* you end up not living with mom anymore?" he asked, stopping again with the ball clutched in his hands. "That's what Denise wanted right... to drop a secret? That's why she said it in front of me and Tim, since I guess we're the only ones who don't know."

"Rod, that shit isn't even relevant to you, don't—"

"Let me decide that," he said, shooting the ball again but not bothering to go running after it. "I wish y'all would stop talking around me like I'm still a kid. I'm sick of everybody except me being in on the big secret."

I raised my hands in front of me. "You'll have to talk to Mom about this, man."

"You know she's not gonna tell me. You're my brother, dude. You're supposed to have my back and you're never even around. But every time I get in trouble, you're the first to tell me how I'm fucking up. What, you can't talk to me about shit unless you can scold me?" he shook his head, muttering something under his breath as he walked back toward the house.

I tipped my head toward the sky, groaning before I called out, stopping him just as he was reaching for the door. "*Alright*, man. But don't say I didn't try to keep you out of it." Trudging over to the patio, I sat down with my back to the table waiting for Rod to join me. "I'm gonna keep this brief," I said, when he dropped into the chair beside me, arms crossed. "Cause I really don't even feel like talking about this shit. Before you were born, obviously, our mom was married to my dad. They got divorced 'cause mom got... sick."

"She was addicted to drugs?"

"What?" I scowled. "*No*. She just had a... a depression problem, and my dad couldn't deal, so they split, and I stayed with her. We moved to a little apartment in the hood, and she went to work and stuff, kept the bills paid, but when she was home... Sometimes she was *on*, you know. Playing, and helping with homework, taking me to the library to play on the computers, shit like that. But sometimes... she wasn't.

She would just go quiet, zone out for days at a time. But we were okay, you know? I took care of her when she got like that, and when she was better, she took care of me. Then she started drinking, and..." I shrugged, slumping in my chair.

"And, what? What happened?"

I ran a thumb over my bottom lip, scratching at the line of stubble that was beginning to grow back. "When I was eleven, she got arrested for a DUI. My dad found out and flipped out, took her to court. Mom gave up... so, I moved in with my dad and stepmom."

"So that's what Denise is holding over her head. Yo... your stepmom is kinda of a bitch."

"Don't call women bitches, Rod." But, I didn't deny his assessment. Mom cleaned herself up, so Denise *was* being ugly by bringing it up. She started seeing a therapist, got a new husband, and right before I turned 14, she had Roderick. Her *new* family, while she left me with my dad and his new wife, and only called once a week, and regularly forgot to call until days after my birthday.

"Whatever. But... mom's not like that anymore, right? She's always been around for me, especially after my dad died."

I huffed, then quickly adjusted the sneer on my face. "Yeah, I know."

"So if you know she's changed, why don't you come around? Mom is cool as hell. Like, she never really trips on me when I mess up."

That's part of the fucking problem.

"I told you man... just busy."

Rod stared at me, and I stared right back, challenging him to call me another liar. I didn't see the benefit for anybody involved if I told him it made me sick to my stomach to see the attention she lavished on Rod, after never bothering to get the help she needed so she could take care of me. Without question, I loved my mom, but I was good on her trying to take on that role *now*, when I was past the point where I needed that from her. I would talk to her on the phone when she called, fine. But I didn't feel like going home and playing her little fantasy perfect family role play. Her visits to me had been few and far between, but it seemed like she was flying out to see Rod every few days. So... yeah, pass.

"Too busy for your damn brother, man?"

I dropped my head, pressing my mouth into a line. Now *that*, I did kinda feel bad about, cause it wasn't Roderick's fault that our mom hadn't been the best for me. Only kind of bad though. Rod was a smart kid, and my mom and his dad gave him the world on a silver fucking platter. He had every advantage for success, and instead he chose to be a borderline delinquent and stay in trouble. I busted my ass for an acceptance to a school my dad and stepmom didn't give a shit about, and busted my ass some more for the scholarships and financial aid to cover the tuition. Rod was lazy as hell, with a college fund thanks to his father.

That was the trade off, I guess. I was coming up on 27 when my father died, and I had plenty of time to know him, plenty of time for his lessons, even if we didn't always agree on the course of my life. I left my IT job to run the shop to honor him. Roderick, on the other hand... he was barely ten when his dad passed. No chance to learn the lessons in manhood, no opportunity to know his dad as not *just* a dad, but a friend.

"I'm sorry man." When I looked at him, he seemed

surprised at those words. "What?" I asked. "Seriously, you're right. You needed somebody. I should have been there, and I let my own shit get in the way. So... I'm sorry."

He nodded. "Okay. I mean... we're good I guess. I just feel like... it's fucked up that I have a brother and we don't even really know each other."

"You're right, man. But hey... you're up here now, and we can fix that. Cool?"

I shook my head, chuckling when a grin spread across his face. "Cool. So... about Viv. Why you ain't tell me you was hitting that? I bet that pus— *ouch*, man. Shit!"

"What? Did I accidentally hit you or something?"

chapter
nine

Carter

"Is this what you would have done to me too?"

I looked up from the computer to glance at Simone, who was sitting on the end of the desk, looking rather uncomfortable with eight months worth of pregnant belly keeping her from sitting straight.

"What are you talking about?" I asked, frowning at the screen as I worked on fixing the mess she'd made of the inventory system I set up for her almost exactly a year ago.

"What you're doing to Viv... Is this what you would have done to me if Roman hadn't been in the picture, and you and I had started dating?"

Gripping the mouse much tighter than necessary, I pretended I didn't see the disappointed look on her face. "What did I do to Viv?"

From the corner of my eye, I could see Simone's expression drift from mild displeasure to outright contempt as she pressed her mouth into a hard line. "Let's see... you treated her like you cared about her, and the minute she tells you she feels the same, you broke her heart."

I knew this was coming. I'd been waiting for it, wondering why it was taking so long for Simone to ride out for her friend. I sat back, studying her as I reclined in the office chair. She had her arms crossed, eyes narrowed... damn, she really was pissed.

"Simone... you know damn well how I feel about Viv."

She rolled her eyes. "Apparently I don't. Apparently, I don't know you that well at all, because the Carter *I* thought I knew wouldn't be playing around with a woman's heart—especially *Viv*. You know what she's been through!"

"How am I playing with her heart? I *never* told her what we were doing was serious. We never even talked about it!"

With difficulty, Simone got down from the desk, hair swinging as she rounded the corner to stand in front of me. "I *know* that. And I told her not to bring it up to you, cause I *knew* you would fuck it up if she did. I *expected* that. What I did *not* expect is that you, knowing how she feels about you and *knowing* that you broke her heart, would sleep with her again."

Oh. That. Probably shouldn't have told her that.

I shook my head, swiping a hand over my face. "I didn't go to her intending for that to happen. I stopped by because I missed my friend, I wanted to see her. *She* initiated sex, not me. And, *by the way*, you know this isn't your business right?"

"*Duh*. But, we're friends, right? So I'm gonna tell you anyway!" She gave an impatient snort as she turned and started pacing the room. "Of course she initiated sex! She misses what you had. Of course she wanted to be with you like that again. *Of course* she's trying to get that closeness back, because she's still emotionally attached, and you don't even have the decency to not pull her back in."

Holding up my hand, I interrupted Simone's rant. "Hold on now, you're not gonna sit here and act like I'm intentionally trying to hurt, or use Viv. You think I'm looking at her like she's just a booty call or something?"

"I know you're not," she said. "That's exactly why this doesn't make any sense to me. If you care for her like you told me you did *two* months ago, you would let her go. Knowing that you're not willing to give her what she needs, you should leave her alone."

"So what, I shouldn't even *talk* to her? Can't even be around her, can't be her damned friend?"

"Carter... you see how that turned out last time, right?"

I scrubbed a hand over my face again, then turned away, pretending to focus on the computer screen. Simone sat down again on the desk, facing me this time, with her head tilted to the side for a long while before she straightened up and spoke.

"You know... I thought you *knew* women, Carter. But the more I learn about you, I don't think that's the case at all. I think you're *very* good at treating women *very* well. I think you're *very* good at taking care of them when they're down. Hell, it's what you did with me, and if it wasn't for Roman...," she paused to shake her head and let out a short huff. "I remember a few months ago, you jokingly told me you had some crazy exes. I wonder how many of those women were women just like me, just like Viv, who you turned on the charm for, loved on them, made them love you, and when they tried to get some type of assurance... you split."

She didn't mean it unkindly, I could tell by her soothing tone, but her words still twisted in my chest like a knife. I guess it must have shown on my face, because she reached over to cover my hand with hers.

"Carter, I'm not trying to make you feel bad, because I don't think you're a bad guy. I *know* you're not a bad guy. I just... don't understand your reluctance to just let someone *love* you. It's okay to do that. But... that's not where you say you are, not what you want from life... so okay. That's fine too. But that's not who Viv is. She *thrives* on love, and if you're not going to facilitate that for her, you need to step aside, and let her move on to someone who will. That can't happen while you're trying to be her "friend".

So... that's what I did.

I hated every minute of it, but I *didn't* call, and I *didn't* text, since it wasn't like she was responding anyway. For two weeks, I was off Viv, cold turkey, and it was only by some type of divine intervention that I didn't see her on the street, or run into her in the halls. She didn't come to me with any complaints about working with Roderick, who honestly seemed to be calming down.

Even though I wasn't seeing her anymore, the way I felt for her didn't die down. In fact, it was almost like the absence made that fullness in my chest intensify to the point that when I finally *did* run into her, early one afternoon at Urban Grind, I felt like my heart might fucking explode. She was sitting in the far corner, flanked on either side by Eddie and Simone. As always, she looked gorgeous... she looked *happy*.

Then, as if she felt me watching her from across the room, she looked up and her eyes met mine. She smiled at me, but then her gaze slid to the right and it faltered as she noticed the pretty woman sitting next to me. Kendra, a hairstylist from the salon next to my shop, was sitting way closer than necessary for a damned coffee date she'd invited herself on, practically in my lap as I ignored whatever she was saying in my ear. She was attractive, yeah, but I wasn't interested, and I was only still beside her because I didn't want to be rude when she spotted me sitting down and asked to join me.

Viv's eyebrow lifted slightly, her nostrils flared just a little, and she returned her eyes back to mine, with a noticeable drop in warmth. The entire exchange took *maybe* ten seconds, and then it was like it never happened. She was warm again, laughing, happy to be having lunch with her friends.

When I saw her get up, heading to the bathrooms, I followed.

"Viv," I called out, catching her before she reached the door. She stopped, and seemed to square her shoulders before she turned around.

"Hello Carter." Her tone was clipped, and even though she was smiling, with her face pulled into a pleasant mask, I could tell she was bothered.

"About Kendra, I—"

"No need to explain," she said, holding up her hands. "You are a single man Carter, you owe me nothing. Who you date is your prerogative."

"I... I just want you to know it's not like that. Not like with me and you."

She smirked, then dropped her gaze to her boots as she

shook her head, then finally looked back up. "For *her* sake, Carter... I certainly hope not."

Then she turned and left me standing in the hall, letting the bathroom door close behind her with a snap.

Well... damn.

I don't know what I expected her reaction to be, but it certainly wasn't *that.* I thought about waiting for her outside, pushing the issue. I didn't want her to think that while *she* was heartbroken, I was moving on, dating, or sleeping with somebody else. Thinking about *that* didn't even feel right. But... maybe this was best. Maybe letting her think I was just an asshole, that I just didn't care... perhaps that's exactly what needed to happen.

***

"I'm pretty sure she asked you to let her go, bruh."

Yeah, so acting like I didn't care was a lot fucking easier said than done, when I walked up the stairs to my floor and found Viv trying, in vain, to pull her wrist from her ex's grip. *Of course* he was the type of bitch-ass dude to try to physically force a woman into doing something. I wasn't even a little bit surprised, but I *was* pissed off, and old boy had about two more seconds to let her go before I snatched his head off.

I was trying to stay calm, not raising my voice, not moving towards them, but apparently he saw danger in my eyes, and he let her go.

"This doesn't even concern you, man," he said, adjusting the collar of his jacket.

"It kinda does, when you're standing in front of my

apartment harassing my neighbor." I finished the last couple of steps, and came to stand in front of him. The intention wasn't *really* to intimidate, but I had at least 50 lbs and 6 inches of height on Darren, so it was a given.

Darren snorted, shooting a scornful look back towards Viv. "He's what... your guard dog or something? Is this what you've been up to, why you won't talk to me now?"

"Yo... Donald—"

"Darren."

I shrugged. "Whatever the hell your name is. Don't talk to her like that. It doesn't look like she's interested, so how about you not talk to her *at all*. How about that?"

He had me several different types of fucked up if he thought I was going to stand here and not say shit while he disrespected Viv. I glanced at her, and she gave a me a little nod of thanks. Just as I was about to return her nod, Darren turned toward the stairs to leave, muttering something under his breath that sounded too much like "fucking slut" for me to let it slide.

I snatched him up by his collar, raising him a little before I shoved him into the wall so I could get right in his face. "Listen, motherfucker. I watched this girl cry over you after *you* fucked up. *You* lied, *you* cheated, *you* were the piece of shit. Don't come around here disrespecting Viv, or I swear to God you will regret the day you ever met her. I oughta toss your ass down these stairs right now."

"Carter... let him go." Viv's hand covered mine, urging me to release my grip on Darren's shirt. I noticed then how tightly I had his collar pulled around his neck, my fist jammed against his throat. His face was slightly red, like he was struggling to breathe. "*Carter*, please. You're hurting him."

I released him abruptly, halfway hoping he would lose his balance and actually take the plunge down the stairs that I threatened. Unfortunately, he didn't, but he didn't say shit else as he scrambled down the steps two at a time. When he was gone, I turned to Viv, my eyes going immediately to her hands as she rubbed her wrist. An ugly bruise was already forming where he grabbed her, and that sight sent a fresh surge of anger rushing through my chest.

"Are you okay?" I asked, reaching for her, but she pulled away.

"Yes." She nodded, but her eyes were glossy and wet like she was on the verge of tears. "Um... thank you for intervening. I only opened the door for him without my pepper spray because I thought he was harmless. He has never touched me like that before. He is... I guess he is very upset because I have not been responding to him."

I shoved my hands in my pockets, desperate to keep them occupied from wanting to touch her. "After the shit he pulled, I don't know why he expected you to do anything but ignore him. What does he want? Did he did think you were going to take him back?"

She shrugged. "I do not know why he thought it was a possibility, but yes, he did. I told him to get his ass off my doorstep."

"Wow. Dude is bold as hell thinking he could still have a place in your life. I can't stand motherfuckers like him."

"Like him?" Viv asked, crossing her arms over his chest.

I nodded. "Yeah. Men that think it's okay to play with

women's emotions, to lie, to trick them into thinking a relationship is something it's not."

Shaking her head, Viv laughed a little, then turned to enter her apartment. Just before she closed the door, she looked me right in the eyes, and asked, "Carter... do you really think you are any better?"

Vivienne

"I believe we may have scared him," I said, laughing through my tears as Roman disappeared through the door, looking very disconcerted by the scene he'd walked in on between Simone and me. We were both crying, sitting cross legged on his living room floor, serving ourselves from a buffet of ice cream on his coffee table.

"Nah," Simone said, balancing her bowl on her leg. "*You* scared him. He's used to me being an emotional mess, especially since the pregnancy. You being all... not happy is new for him I think. But... I mean, you're managing a *lot* right now emotionally. Are you sure you're okay? Do you want me to ask Roman to kick Carter's ass? I asked once already, but I think he thought I was playing."

I laughed again, wiping my face dry with the back of my hand. "That is not necessary." Simone rolled her eyes, then took another dramatic spoonful of ice cream. "*Seriously*," I said. "I do not even understand why I still needed to come here for this, you know? It's like... I can't just ignore the hurt like I want to."

"Well... Viv, you never gave yourself a chance to really get over what Darren did. You "ignored" the hurt and got wrapped up in Carter. And based on what you told me about your little scandal in France, you did the same thing with Thierry, just came over here and immersed yourself in work, never giving yourself a chance to work through it. So... what you're feeling now is the result of *three* broken hearts."

I heaved a sigh, throwing my head back against the seat of the couch. "So what do I do?"

"What every other woman does, I guess," Simone said with a shrug. "You *hurt*. You be a little mean to the person that did it, and you sit on the floor and eat ice cream with your pregnant friend, and then, eventually you move on. You heal. Maybe with the help of a lover, maybe not."

"So you think I should go on a date?"

"Maybe so."

I scoffed. "Maybe *not*. I actually... I don't know, the last month, even though I've been emotional, I've actually felt like I could catch my breath...learning to enjoy my own company again, you know?"

Simone smiled. "Yeah. I do."

A comfortable silence settled between us as we finished our ice cream, then Simone asked, "Have you talked to Carter lately?"

"No," I answered, ignoring the slight increase in my heart rate. "Not since that little incident two weeks ago where he nearly killed Darren." I shook my head, wondering where Darren had found the ridiculous amount of nerve required to think that I would take him back. His sob story, about yet another makeup and breakup with his fiancé was compelling, but I had absolutely no interest in him, not anymore. After I made *that* clear, he decided to get ugly, but then Carter came along. "I am still wondering why he has the idea that what he did to me was somehow better than

Darren."

Simone lifted an eyebrow. "You really think that, Viv?"

"It had the same result, so yes."

Simone frowned, absently scraping her spoon around her empty bowl.

"I'm guessing you disagree?" She gave me a sheepish smile, but still said nothing. "Simone," I urged, "Say what you need to say. We are friends. You can tell me if you see this differently."

"I do," she nodded. "I mean... I understand that he was sending you mixed signals. I totally, *totally* get that he hurt you, and trust me, I've torn into his ass about that. But he never lied to you Viv. He never treated you like you were second rate, never intentionally used words to cut you, not like Darren did. Darren... that motherfucker is a snake. I just don't think Carter fits into that category."

I sucked my teeth. "You say he has never lied, but all those loving words, brushing my hair, rubbing my feet... do you know he went and bought tampons for me once? In retrospect, *all* of that was a lie. He was doing all of those things to make me think he cared, when truly, he did not. Not in the way he tried to make me believe."

"That's not true," Simone said, lifting a finger. "*That*, I know for a fact. I know that him hurting you makes it hard to believe, but Carter *absolutely* cares for you."

"Then what is the problem?"

Simone sighed, looking up at the ceiling for a moment before she brought her head back down. "Carter... is not who you think you're gonna get when you *look* at Carter. Outwardly, he seems like this very put together, very confident guy, right? But... he's not. Or at least, *he* doesn't see it that way. Has he talked to you about his mom, about his family before?"

"A little bit... not too much detail though. I could tell it was a sensitive subject."

She nodded. "Well, it's not my story to tell, so I'm not going to tell it, *but*... I can say that I think Carter has a whole lot of self-doubt that came out of that. Because of it... I think he has a hard time accepting love. He *gives* it very naturally — you and he have that in common. I mean... even with *Roman,* after the miscarriage, you know how he was there for him and they were just kind of... homeboys, you know? Not exactly friends, especially when they were rivaling for my attention — which, by the way, was *only* because you were unavailable. Carter has *always* had a crush on you. But, anyway, after that, because Carter is just that kind of guy, they became friends. So when you guys came together, these two huge-hearted people, it was like kismet, you know? You and he both shared with me how *beautiful* it felt. But... you had your doubts that he felt the same, and I don't think it mattered to Carter if you felt the same or not. It wasn't even on his radar, he was just happy to have somebody to love on... while trying to convince himself that's not what was happening."

I remained quiet, simply absorbing Simone's words as she continued.

"And then *you*, after I *told* you... *begged* you not to... you had to go and ask for a definition. Don't get me wrong... I understand why you needed one, but I knew you were gonna scare the shit out him, and he was gonna be like "whoa, stop the presses." Now... it's not that I don't think he was wrong for getting *so* involved with you when he had so much uncertainty rolling around, I do. And then the fact that he was so inarticulate about it, and he kept trying to be so close to you, my God... I kinda wanted to stab him in the chest, seriously. Just a shallow wound though, nothing fatal. *And* in the sake of fairness, I do want to reiterate that *sleeping with someone you're trying to get over is not a smart thing to do.*"

I rolled my eyes as she playfully nudged me with her foot, but I knew for a fact *that* was true. That night, I'd had a few glasses of wine, and I was feeling terribly lonely, and missing Carter *so* bad. And then there he was at my door. I didn't invite him in intending to sleep with him, but once we were together, it felt so much like old times that when the urge hit to kiss him.. I did. Because that's just what was natural between us. There was a moment, standing in my mirror, where I knew it was a mistake, knew we shouldn't go there again when I wanted something he didn't... but our eyes met, and no matter what his *mouth* said... I saw love there.

Afterwards... reality came back.

"But, *anyway,*" Simone continued, "I've already said *way* too much, but it's only because I kinda still hope there's a chance for you guys."

I shook my head. "I don't know Simone. I may give my heart easily, but you only have to break it once for me to learn my lesson about *you*."

"And I get that, I totally do. Just... maybe keep an open mind."

Carter

Twelve. Thirteen. Fourteen. Fifteen.

The strain ripping through my biceps didn't mean

anything to me as I lifted the weight over my chest, lowered, then repeated. Sweat dripping in my eyes, the corrugated metal bar biting into my hands because I forgot my gloves, nothing fucking mattered. Viv thought I was just as bad as fucking *Darren*, and that didn't sit well with me at all.

"You're gonna regret that in two days," Roman said, entering the weights area from the direction of the locker rooms. He smirked as he passed me, kneeling to adjust the weights on the machine I'd just finished using.

I knew he was right. If I kept it up, I would wake up in two days stiff and sore, barely able to move because I'd over-worked my muscles, and I wouldn't have anybody to blame but myself. I pushed the bar back up onto the rack and sat up, using my tee-shirt to wipe my face.

Roman shook his head as he grabbed the handlebar for his machine, positioning himself in front of it to do bicep curls. "So," he said, glancing at me as he pulled up the weight. "What's been going on with you man? You haven't been around lately, not even at the barbershop. What's up?"

I shrugged, leaning to grab the bottle of water at my feet. "Nothing man. Just laying low."

"Mm. Would that have anything to do with a falling out with a certain chocolate shop owner?"

"Maybe... maybe not."

Roman laughed. "So you mean it definitely does. Carter... dude, what's your problem? You're falling apart on me, man. What the fuck did you and Viv do to each other?"

"What are you talking about?" I asked, lifting an eyebrow.

"You're all moody and shit lately. *She's* all moody and shit lately. Right now, Viv is in *my* living room with Simone, eating up my little girl's ice cream, and crying and shit, and I heard your name. Simone actually asked me to kick your ass a few weeks ago. So... what did you do?"

I took a swig from my water. "Nothing."

"Bullshit," Roman said, finishing his first set of reps. He stepped back, glancing at his watch to time his break. "You forget that I've known you for years, Carter. I've seen you with women. Heard you talk about women. You and Viv... that was some whole other, next level shit. Never seen you like that with anybody else. So... I ask again... what happened?"

"She wanted something I couldn't give."

Roman cocked his head to the side, then huffed as he bent to pick up the handlebar again. "Why not?" he asked, as he began his second round of bicep curls. "I'm assuming she wanted what, a relationship? So why not? You're about to be 32 years old man, we're not kids anymore. Why not Viv?"

"Why not anybody?" I tossed my hands into the air in a defeated gesture, then swiped one over my face. "I wasn't looking for that with anybody. I don't even have my own shit together, plus I've got my little brother up here to worry about. And Viv... damn, man. Viv is fucking *amazing*, but I can't go there. Not with her."

"But you *went* there, already. From what I could see that was damn near your wife for a good month, month and a half, so what changed? You were cool with the arrangement as long as you didn't *talk* about the arrangement?"

I shook my head. "No, it wasn't that. Like... when I first talked to Viv after she broke up with old boy, it was just about cheering her up, making her smile, making her laugh. But then, we just... we *vibed*, and I wanted to be around her all the time. Viv is the kind of woman that you don't mean to get caught up in, but before you know it, you're stuck, and you can't pull yourself out. You're catching feelings when you didn't even intend to, and then once we slept together... ." I groaned, reaching up to massage the back of my neck. "I was okay with feeling like I did about her. Didn't mind that at all. But... Viv has had her heart broken, like... ripped out of her chest and stomped type of broken. She told me she was putting her heart on the line, and... I just couldn't do it anymore."

"Why not?" Roman asked, cleaning off the handlebar as he finished with the weight machine. "You went after Simone... Why not Viv? You scared of a girl with a broken heart?"

"Hell yes," I said, chuckling. "Simone... she was — no disrespect intended — *easy*. And I don't mean that like I could have easily had sex with her or anything like that, I mean emotionally, Simone was strong. She wasn't putting up with any bullshit, she wasn't fractured... she didn't have the kind of cracks that Viv does. Man... the way I feel about Viv, I... I don't ever wanna be responsible for the kind of tears I've seen her shed because she was hurting. But I ended up doing it anyway, and now... hell, I'm just trying not to make the shit any worse. I don't want to let her down like that again."

Roman stared at me, frowning, for a long moment before he shook his head. "Carter...you know... that's your fucking problem, right there. You're worried about letting your stepmom and deceased father down, so instead of doing what *you* wanna do with your life, you run and work in a barbershop when you don't even like cutting hair. You were worried about letting your little brother down, so you... I don't know, decided to just not be around. You and Viv catch feelings for each other, and you don't wanna let *her* down.... so you break it off with her. You're doing some pretty disappointing shit for the sake of not disappointing anybody."

"So what am I supposed to do then?"

"*Something else*, genius. You've never heard that doing the same thing over and over, expecting a different result is the definition of insanity? You're sick of the barbershop, you wanna work in technology... do it. You want a better relationship with your brother... make it happen. You like Viv, wanna be with her... just *do it*. It's not that fucking hard, man."

Roman gave me a brotherly pat on the shoulder, then went across the room to use a different machine, but I was done. I hit the showers, then left, with his words resonating in my head the entire way home. Maybe I had, without realizing it, become stagnant, stuck in a cycle of non-action. *Maybe* that's why being with Viv had been such a breath of fresh air. She was different, and beautiful, and... probably exactly what I needed, and I fucked it up.

That's what I should have been asking Roman's advice about. He was the king of getting his girl back, after all of the ups and downs he had gone through with Simone. Maybe if I took a page out of his book, I could turn things between Viv and me around... but I didn't know if she was even still willing to trust me like that.

Career-wise... I had no doubts that I could thrive in the tech market. That's where my passion was, it's what I did, but the barbershop... that was family. Those were my roots. Before the neighborhood had been cleaned up and turned into the black business mecca that it was now, I would go to the shop after school, back when it was still simply named "pops", and sweep up hair to earn money to pay for internet access at home. I grew up here, watching my grandfather, then my dad turn this into a spot to not just get your hair cut, but gain a community. *That's* what I enjoyed. Not the trip to barbering college at my dad's insistence, and definitely not cutting hair. I was good at it, sure, but it wasn't where my heart was.

When I walked into my apartment, Roderick was sitting on my couch, holding a large canvas in front of him and staring at it in awe. "Hey... what's that?" I asked, taking of my coat to hang on the hook by the door.

"Heaven," he answered, his face spreading into a euphoric grin.

I narrowed my eyes, stepping around to the back of the couch to look at the front of the canvas.

Motherfucker.

I snatched the print of my *favorite* picture of Viv, the one with her covered in caramel, from his hands, clutching it against me to hide it from his view. "Where the fuck did you get this man?"

"Delivery man. It was here when I got home."

"Did it have *your* name on the packaging?"

He reached up, scratching his eyebrow. "Well... not *technically*, meaning... no, not at all."

Groaning, I carefully lowered the picture, propping it against the wall so that the back was facing out. "Where's the damn packaging, Rod?"

"On the counter."

I shuffled through the thick brown paper on the counter,

searching for something that would tell me where the pictures had come from. When I found the packing slip, I scanned it for the purchase date.

Just over a month ago, billed to Vivienne Lambert. I dropped the slip onto the counter, massaging my temples. There was no way I could keep a gift like this from her, but... how could I return it without being awkward?

Out of the corner of my eye, I saw Roderick trying to sneak over to look at the picture again, and I grabbed him by the back of his collar, tugging him away. "Show some respect man, she's your boss."

"I know, and I will be at work *early* tomorrow."

I shook my head, pushing him back into the living room as I picked up the picture to place safely in my bedroom. Obsessing over that could wait until later.

"Alright, I said, re-entering the living room and pulling the XBOX controller from Rod's hands. "It's time to do another progress check, since you've got free time to play video games."

Roderick scowled, but he was paying attention. "Alright. What's up?"

"You still doing alright on the job with Viv?"

"Yeah."

"Not running her nerves into the ground?"

"Nah, man. Viv likes me. She says I work hard."

I nodded. "Good. You got a test date for your GED yet?"

"Yeah. It's gonna take all day, but I'm scheduled."

"Okay... good. You been looking at colleges?"

"Already picked one out."

I pulled my head back as a smile spread across my face.

"That's good man. So... you really are serious, aren't you?" I asked, leaning back into the couch cushions.

He shrugged, but I picked up on the smile playing at the corners of his mouth.

"What about this girl you've been seeing... you serious about her?"

I got another hunch of his shoulders, but he was having a harder time maintaining a serious expression.

"Okay, I won't push. You can keep it to yourself. Just... make sure you're using condoms dude, 'cause you can't have a girl and a baby moving in here."

"I know. We're... we're being careful."

"Good. I'ma let you get back to your game."

I handed him back the control and headed to my room.

"Hey... Carter," Roderick said, turning to look at me across the back of the couch.

"Yeah? What's up?"

"Thanks, man. For... letting me come up here with you, looking out for me. I appreciate it, for real."

I grinned, giving him a two-finger salute. "Hey, that's the point of having a brother, right?"

He returned my salute with a nod, then turned back to his game. I closed the door behind me to tune out the sound of him killing zombies or whatever he was doing, so I could focus on how to handle the delicacy of returning the picture to Viv. I even texted Simone, and didn't get a response, which didn't surprise me, because it was late, and pregnancy had been kicking her butt. She was probably asleep. Finally, after spending an hour coming up with crazy solutions, all of which led back to her probably being pissed, I decided to just approach it head on, and be honest. So I texted *her*.

"Hey Viv. I got this print you ordered for me, I'm assuming as a gift. I don't know if it would be weird/creepy for me to keep it, but I didn't want to return it to you with no explanation or to be misinterpreted. I know this is awkward, but... please tell me what do."

Too late, I remembered that Roman had told me that she and Simone were having the equivalent of an adult sleepover, and had undoubtedly spent a good part of the night clowning *me*.

Shit.

I was using my phone to google how to delete a text message from somebody else's phone when her response popped up on the screen.

"It was intended as a gift, so please accept it as such. I do not think that is weird/creepy at all. Consider it something to remember me by :) — Frenchy."

Okay, so she was in a good mood, and she had actually sent back a response. But... what did I say back now? I couldn't leave it up in the air. I knew enough about women to know that you *always* make yours the last response, you never leave them hanging.

But what the fuck do I say?

It was weird between us now. I didn't want to say anything too overtly affectionate, but I also didn't want to seem dry.

"Thank you, I will. I hope you're doing okay."

That worked. Simple, but it left the door open for a little more.

"I am. Thank you for asking. You? — Frenchy."

"Glad to hear it. I'm okay too."

"That is good to know. Really. Good night, Carter. — Frenchy."

"Good night."

chapter
ten

Vivienne

"SIT UP STRAIGHT. WE ARE AT THE DINNER TABLE, not in a pig sty."

I stopped chewing and rolled my eyes. Of *course* it did not matter to my father that after a long day on my feet in the kitchen at Guilty Pleasures, I was tired. It was irrelevant — to him — that he and my mother had popped up in the middle of the week for a surprise visit, interrupting my own dinner plans of a bottle of wine and the italian sausage calzone now getting cold on my counter, both consumed in a hot bubble bath, with my headphones in my ears. What was important, apparently, was that I used proper posture at my tiny dining room table, with me and my parents the only guests in attendance.

"Leave her alone, Martin, she is at home," my mother said, smiling at me from across the table.

My father snorted. "So it is okay to be a slob at home? I did not realize. Perhaps I should no longer be berated about my socks on the floor, *non*?"

The cheerful smile slid from my mother's face, quickly

replaced by pinched lips. She opened her mouth to speak, but I raised a hand, waving her off. "It is okay, Mère, I do not mind sitting up. Although, I am unsure how Père is able to notice my proper posture — or lack thereof— anyway, since he has barely even looked up from his Blackberry long enough to enjoy the meal he insisted I cook."

I ignored the looks of shock from both of my parents as I drained my wine glass, then reached for the bottle to pour myself another glass of the $200 Bordeaux my mother had placed in my hands on the way in.

"I think you've had too much," my father said, his voice low and measured as he spoke.

My nostrils flared. "Au contraire, Père. I assure you, I've not had nearly enough. I am exhausted, physically and emotionally. The wine was a gift for the hostess, correct? Since that unlucky, involuntary person is me, I will drink the whole bottle if I wish."

"*Se taire, fille*, you will *not* speak to me this way."

"Then do not speak to *me* as if I am a child," I countered, ignoring the fist he slammed on the table.

"Then do not *act* as one, chéri. Complaining of emotional exhaustion — from *what*, might I ask? Because we emigrated you here to work, to make a living, not to exhaust your emotions."

I didn't respond, jabbing instead at a stray morsel of food on my plate.

My mother's gaze bored against me, and when I did not look up, she drew in an audibly sharp breath. "*Merde*," she muttered under her breath. Then louder, she said, "Let me guess... the neighbor?"

Running my tongue over my teeth, I finally looked up,

nodding as I looked between them. "But no fear, mère et mon père, there is no scandal this time. No need to banish me to another country just for a little broken heart."

"*Banish*?" My mother recoiled, as if she'd been slapped. "Vivi, you make it sound as if it was a punishment!"

I snorted. "Was it *not*? I get taken advantage of, and the first thing you do is pack me up and ship me away."

"For you *protection*, Vivi," my father chimed in, strain evident in both his face and voice. "Thierry Girard was infamous for his exploits in the French financial markets, both lawful and criminal. We were trying to get you away from that! While you were using my credit to decorate your new American apartment, journalists and photographers knocked at our doors, requesting comment on your status as Girard's mistress. *Dieu merci* that this was ten years ago and not today, where some website would be dragging your reputation through the mud and people with cell phone cameras would be stalking you on your walk to work."

I swallowed hard, then took a deep breath, finishing my glass of wine in one gulp before I spoke. "I did not know."

"Really?" He asked with a snort. "Is *that* why you are impertinent enough to speak to me as if I am the gardener? Morgan, do you see? We have raised a child who does not recognize or appreciate even *half* of the things we have done for her. The best schools, designer wardrobes, gourmet snacks for playdates, luxury cars for her to destroy while learning to drive... Perhaps we have done too much, if she has so much leisure time for the collection of romance and hurt feelings."

In my lap, I clenched my hands into fists so tight that my nails bit into my skin. "You act as if I am *nothing*. As if I've *done* nothing. I maintained impeccable grades throughout my years of schooling, no tutors. Excelled at every extra-curricular I was given. Received top honors at university. I have never been arrested, never touched an illicit drug. I live off the salary I *earn* from the successful business I've built. *This* apartment? I paid for, furnished from my own pocket. And before you say this is only because I am your child, given the privilege to work in your business, please recall that I was hired on *merit*. I am no spoiled princess, living off my family's name. I was no "daddy's little girl". My childhood was not one of hugs and kisses from you, or sitting on your knee. Since I was a little girl, you have pushed and pushed, demanded hard work, and every single time, I have met, and exceeded the challenge. Do not misrepresent me as some foolish girl only getting by on a pretty face."

"Ah, so you are not a simpleton after all, there is some fire there. Very good. *But*, appreciate who stoked that flame in you, hmm? Do you think you cultivated this intrepid spirit on your own? *Non*. We could not have you running around, a beautiful, free-hearted girl with no sense. Because you understand that's what you would be had we not demanded more?"

"*Martin*. Enough." My mother rested her hand on my father's, quieting his rant. I reached for my water, desperate for something to soothe the fire burning in my chest and on my face because of my father's harsh words.

"Vivi." His voice was noticeably softer under my mother's influence, and I looked up, clutching the icy cold glass to my chest as the condensation pruned my fingers. "I do not mean to upset you. I love you, but I have no patience for this foolishness. The affairs, the nose piercing, those *pictures*...

you are a brilliant girl, yet you are ruled by emotion instead of your brain, and this is something I do not understand."

I pressed my lips together in an effort to calm my trembling chin, then shook my head. "I do not need your understanding, papa. Only your love."

"You have it."

"Do I? Your way of showing it is foreign to me. It seems to me that I am such a disappointment in your eyes that I cannot afford the extravagance of making mistakes, or having my heart broken, or heaven forbid, being sexy and having fun. I am young and healthy, it is what I *should* be doing. If I am being otherwise responsible, I do not see the problem. If you are not okay with my life... it is *not* my problem, not anymore. I am thirty years old... I cannot live under the shadow of your expectations forever." I barely held in a laugh at the irony of me declaring myself an adult, when this whole conversation was started by me throwing a tantrum like an over-tired toddler.

"I am sorry, Vivi," my father said, coming to kneel beside my chair. When I turned to face him, he took my head in his hands and kissed my forehead, then both cheeks. "You are right... perhaps I am expecting too much of *me* in you. Please, mon trésor, do not ever doubt that I love you. You and your mother... you are what I live for. Comprendre?"

I nodded, giving up on holding back my tears as he pulled me into his arms. I stayed there for a long time. This was such a rare occurrence that I didn't want to let go, but as usual, my parents were only stopping through as they jet-set around the world. When they left, I was not sad. I was very, very full, happier than I'd felt in the entire month since the loss of my friendship with Carter.

***

Mid-afternoon the day after my parents' visit, I was jolted awake by someone knocking at my door. Still groggy, I dragged myself out of bed, and went to the door, lifting myself up on my toes to see through the peephole.

Carter!

"Just a moment," I yelled, suddenly *very* awake, and aware that I was *very* naked. I ran back to my room, where I pulled a tee shirt over my head and yanked on a pair of yoga pants, then returned to the door.

Oh my.

I knew that absence supposedly made the heart grow fonder, but... was there an equivalent for the throbbing between your thighs when you came back in contact with someone who used to make your body feel very, *very* good? His shoulders seemed wider, he seemed taller, his skin smoother, his face more handsome than it had been just a week ago. Like I was seeing him as he was before everything went wrong.

Carter just stood there for a moment, staring, before a smile began to play at the corners of his mouth.

"What is so funny?" I asked, placing a hand on my hip.

He pointed up to my hair, finally breaking into a full grin. "You've got a wine cork in your hair."

My eyes went wide, and my hands went immediately into my hair to find and remove the cork. "What can I say, it was a wild night," I said dryly, chuckling as I tossed it between my hands. The truth was that I'd uncorked the bottle while I was sitting in the bed, already half-asleep. I passed out before I had a single glass of the sure-to-be-ruined wine. "So... did you want something?"

"Um... yeah. Roman and Simone said they've been trying to call you... she went into labor about an hour ago."

I gasped, bringing my hand up to my chest. "*What*? Are you serious! My goodness!" I turned and headed back into my apartment, wondering what in the world I'd done with my phone. "Don't just stand there, you are letting the cold in from the hall. Come in, and close the door!"

Carter hesitated, and I could see the uncertainty playing on his face before he finally did step in, closing the door behind him. He hovered there, with his hands shoved in the pockets of his sweatpants as I dumped my purse on the counter, looking for my phone.

It was one of the last items to fall out, and it was so dead that it didn't even immediately respond when I plugged it into my kitchen charger. I groaned, remembering that it had been low when I left work the previous evening, and my parents' surprise appearance at my door had disrupted me from making sure it ended up on the charger.

"So, tell me what happened, is she doing okay, will the baby be here soon? How did she look?" I asked, leaving the phone in the kitchen and motioning for him to follow me into my room.

"Um... I don't know how she looked," Carter said, stopping at the door to my bathroom as I pulled out a brush to tackle my hair into a bun. "I haven't been to the hospital."

I paused, with the brush in midair. "Really? Why not?"

He shook his head. "I uh, I don't *do* hospitals. Spent way too much time in them when my dad was sick."

"*Oh*. That is understandable," I said, nodding as I

finished fixing my hair. "You never told me what was wrong with him."

"Prostate cancer. He was in treatment a long time, then that stopped working,... then hospice care... So, yeah, no hospitals for me unless I'm on the gurney."

"I see. I'm very sorry you went through that."

Our eyes met in the mirror, and he tried to force a smile, but it turned into more of a grimace. Unsure of what to say next, I occupied my mouth by brushing my teeth while he updated me on Simone's status, as relayed to him by Roman.

After I'd washed my face, he followed me into my room, hovering near the door while I pulled out weather appropriate clothes for the snow that had been falling for the last few days. I yanked off my tee shirt, and was pulling the straps of a bra over my shoulders when I realized that I'd just stripped half-naked in front of Carter.

Clutching the bra to my chest, I slowly turned my eyes to where he was, simultaneously disappointed and relieved that he was turned toward the hall, resting his shoulder in the doorframe. It was an incredibly strange feeling. On one hand, I was glad he was respectful enough to recognize my oversight when I did not, and not take advantage of my absent mindedness. On the other hand, I think a little part of me was almost disappointed that he was able to resist, when just a little over a month ago, he could not keep his eyes off me.

Shaking both thoughts from my head, I dressed quickly, then tapped him on the shoulder to let me pass, so that I could retrieve my phone from the kitchen.

"Thank you for coming to let me know," I said, restocking my purse as I stood at the counter. "I do not know how long I would have slept, or how long it would have taken me to realize I was without a phone. I would have never forgiven myself for not being available for Simone."

He smiled, and *damnit*, warmth washed through me with the strength of a tropical storm wave. "Yeah, I kinda figured that. I was a little scared you weren't gonna answer for me and I was gonna have to just shout it to you through the door, but I manned up," he said with a chuckle. "But nah, seriously... It was no hassle. It's what friends do, right?"

I returned his smile, then nodded. "Yes. That is what friends do."

***

IS ONE NIGHT OF UNINTERRUPTED SLEEP SIMPLY too much to ask?

A yawn overtook me as I trudged to the front door, cursing whoever was interrupting my plans of turning in early. Roderick had tried his best to convince me to come to Urban Grind with him, insisting that I just *had* to dance with him at least one time. But, I had other things in store for myself. The idea was that by going to bed at ten, with my alarm set for eight the next morning, I could get a full ten hours of sleep to make up for the week I'd spent staying up late and waking early. But, that plan was out, thanks to someone banging on my door at midnight with what seemed to be increasing persistence. I groaned at who I saw on the other side of the peephole.

"Eddie," I said, eyebrow lifted as I opened the door. "I would think that *you* of all people, would let me get my rest.

Did you not drag me over the coals about the bags under my eyes not even two days ago?"

"But you look so pretty now," he said, briefly cupping my chin before slipping past me.

With a little sigh, I closed the door, locking it behind me as I headed to the kitchen, where Eddie was already pulling a bottle of wine from my cooler. "To what do I owe the pleasure of your company at nearly midnight on the weekend?"

Eddie stopped his uncorking process to shoot me a smile. "Gimme just a second, you'll see. I can't stay long, because I have a date, but I have something I want to show you."

"A date, Eddie? It is the middle of the night!"

"What's your point?"

I opened my mouth, then stopped, shaking my head. "I guess I have none. We are adults, no curfew."

"That's right. I ran into a group of four of the *finest* women I've ever seen on the way over here. They said they're having a bachelorette's night out... asked me to join. The future bride, in particular wanted to have some... *fun*." Eddie gave me a grin. "I told little miss bride-to-be Kelly we could definitely have some fun."

I cocked my head to the side. "The night before her wedding, Eddie? That's terrible!"

"No, what's terrible is having a wedding this time of year anyway, when it's cold and gloomy like this. But, hey... if she's not mad, neither am I. Besides, her future husband isn't shit anyway, and she knows it. They keep making up, breaking up, you know how it goes. She's one of *those* girls, who just wants the ring anyway."

"How do you know her man is not... wait a minute... *Kelly*? Eddie..."

Kelly and Darren's engagement turn up... no way, can't be...

He grinned, giving me a sly wink. "Hold that thought for *after* this, okay?"

A few minutes later, we were seated together on my couch, wine in hand as Eddie pulled out his cell phone and turned on the screen. He held it up in front of us and turned up the volume.

Immediately, I recognized the place on the screen as Urban Grind, converted to the nighttime set up for Open Mic. What surprised me was the fact that Carter was on stage, with a mic perched in front of him, looking handsome, but not quite as laid-back as usual.

"Oh my God, he is so fine! I would wrap my hands up in those locs, and—"

"Girl, that man doesn't want you. He's spoken for, get your life."

I gasped when I realized that was Eddie snapping at some poor innocent woman in the crowd. "Eddie, *why* did you do her like that?"

He shrugged. "I was tired of her, she wanted to take *everybody* home."

"And *you* are judging her for this?" I asked, lifting an eyebrow.

"Focus on what matters," he said, with a sly grin. "Did you know he was a little wannabe *Verses and Flow* artist?" When I didn't respond, he sucked his teeth at my blank expression. "I forgot. Americanized, my ass. Poetry, Viv. Did you know he did poetry?"

"Oh! Yes, yes I did. Is that what is about to happen?" I asked, turning my eyes back to the screen. From the technicians behind him on stage, and the lights brought up to full brightness, I presumed that something had gone wrong with the sound system between performances, and Carter was waiting to start.

"You're about to see."

I held my breath as the lights went low, and the extra people exited the stage. Carter stepped up to the front of the stage, giving the crowd an easy, charming smile that made several people — mostly women — catcall in appreciation. He responded to that with another grin, an embarrassed one this time, and *that* only made them get louder.

"Would y'all *stop*? What, y'all tryna make me blush or something?" he asked, in that low sexy voice, and that was maybe a mistake, because there was a bit of a collective gasp, followed by a dull cacophony as the audience struggled with the apparent *need* to talk about him, and a desire to not make him nervous. As if they *could* make him nervous.

I thought I knew better, but really, watching him on screen instead of being mesmerized by his real, physical presence... Carter *didn't* look that relaxed. His hands were shoved in his pockets when he wasn't using one to rub the back of his neck, I could see the tension in his shoulders, and his eyes held the tiniest hint of anxiety. But then he shook his head, smiled again, and cool, composed Carter was back.

"So... I'm no Langston Hughes, but I do a little bit of writing... nothing that was ever really intended to share with the public, so it's not the most polished, not perfect. But... it's from the heart, and I've got somebody looking up to me that has something he's scared—"

"I ain't scared!" I heard Roderick call out from somewhere in the crowd, gaining a smattering of laughter and applause.

"Alright," Carter said, chuckling. "Apprehensive, then. Does that work?" he asked, and presumably got an affirmative response from Rod, because he shook his head and continued. "Anyway, *that*," — he pointed to Rod — "little motherfucker dared me to do something *I* was... apprehensive... about, because how I could encourage him to face *his* fears if I couldn't face my own? So I'm doing exactly that, because adults know that if you want kids to eat their broccoli, you gotta eat yours first. So... here we go. This is called, *The Gift*."

"I cannot watch this," I said, tapping the screen of Eddie's phone to pause the video. "My hands are so sweaty, I feel so... *nervous*."

Eddie scowled at me. "*Why*?"

"I don't know." I frowned. "I just... I know his writing was very private for him, this feels like an invasion of that."

"He recited it in front of a crowd, Viv. I'm pretty sure he understood that people were gonna hear it. *You* need to hear it. I didn't use up all this good memory on my phone recording this for you to *not* watch."

Eddie took the phone from me and hit play again, propping it against the stack of hardbound confectionery cookbooks on the coffee table so we could both see. My heart started racing, and butterflies went wild in my belly the moment Carter spoke his first words.

"My heart's not on my sleeve, so she thinks I don't care

Always thought actions spoke louder than words, but she'd rather hear it

But how do you put into words what doesn't make sense in

your head,

That she came out of nowhere, with her heart in shambles
Didn't ask me to fix it, didn't ask for first aid
But... how could I not try to ease her pain?"

"Uh-uh," I said, shaking my head as I paused it again. My heart was somewhere around my throat, stomach churning as I processed Carter's words.

"What's the problem?" Eddie asked, as I lifted my glass to take a long gulp of wine.

I finished that glass and reached for the bottle to pour another. "What's the problem? Are you serious? This is about me!"

Eddie sucked his teeth. "Um... Ms. Conceited, you don't know that."

Pausing with my glass in midair, I let that bounce around in my mind. I *didn't* know that. This could be about any number of women from Carter's past... or present. Or, completely fictional. I didn't "know" it was about me.

"So can we continue, please?"

With a deep breath, and another deep swig from my glass, I nodded.

"She's beautiful, and free, fresh air personified
The kind of ambush on your soul that you see from a mile back but run in anyway,
Willingly, gladly, you get all the way into this trap
Cause there's a piece right there that's broken
And you know how to mend it
You've been cleaning up that kind of mess since you were just a little dude
You didn't even fully understand how big the wreckage was

But you found out that some damage needs a specialist

And once it's cleaned up, you're no longer needed

So you go for the ones that are uncomplicated

Cause all you have in the back of your mind is the one you loved first

The one you loved hardest, before you even knew what that was

Before you even knew who you *were.*

The one you fixed over and over until you couldn't keep up...

And then... well, you've lost your usefulness.. haven't you?

So they abandon you

They give you up

Cause who wants a junior repairman who can't keep it together when the cops come?"

I paused the video again, turning to Eddie with drooping shoulders and a trembling chin.

"I know," he nodded, his own voice sounding distinctly thick. "Not a dry eye in the house."

Placing my glass on the table, I wiped my eyes with the back of my hand, unsurprised that I felt an overwhelming need to go and knock on Carter's door.

"Let's go ahead and finish it, okay?" Eddie asked, gesturing at the screen. I didn't respond, just bit my lip as I looked away, and a few seconds later, Carter's voice filled the room again, through the speakers of the phone.

"So yeah, you stuck to the ones who didn't need that from you

Intact, undamaged, no snags to keep you boxed in and hooked on the kind of all-consuming love that only a woman like that has...

But then you see her, *and you can't help it, cause...* damn... *did you see her?*

Beautiful, broken-hearted girl, in need of mending

And you know you should run in the other direction

*But you can't, because...*damn...*did you see her?*

And before you know what happened, man, she's fixing you

Filling up places you didn't know were empty with energy and light

Warning you not to let the pretty face fool you cause she knows her shit

Opening her door for you at three in the morning cause she knows you need her to sleep

And turning you on without even trying

And making you think about shit like what you would name your kids,

And... putting her heart on the line even though you didn't ask

Hell, you didn't even know she *was feeling like* that

Cause remember... you're *the one that's used to doing all the repairs*

So when she wants to do some building of her own, you don't know how to accept it...

So you don't.

So... I guess it's not really a surprise that she thinks I don't care

When I rejected her offering and selfishly wanted to still be only her "friend"

Even though a "friend" is the last damn thing I want to "only" be

But I can't give her those words

Can't put it out there like that

Because she — he stopped to laugh — *she's got interesting adornments*

in interesting places

And she's brilliant, and feisty, and successful

And she's funny, and she's beautiful, and stronger than she knows

But then you look at yourself

And it doesn't even feel like you've got your shit together

And the times when you feel like you're *enough aren't enough*

And you can't find the words to just tell her *that, so instead... you push her away*

Cause you didn't ask for her heart, remember?"

"I cannot do this," I said, tapping the screen as I swallowed hard to clear my throat. "I cannot—"

Eddie put a hand on my shoulder. "He's almost finished. Just listen."

"But... retrospect is the clearest lens to view life,

the only way to filter through the bullshit and excuses

that you don't even know you're wallowing in until you're on the other side

Nevertheless, you only have to break her heart once for her to never forget

So I can only hope that one day she can take a chance, and extend it again

And that *time... I'll shut the fuck up and accept my gift."*

The crowd erupted in snaps, complete with a few whistles, some cheers, and more than a couple of people shouted invitations to "make him feel better", but Carter left the stage with no fanfare. The video ended, and Eddie turned to me, reaching forward to wipe tears from my face.

"So... tell me, Viv. After hearing *that*... are you feeling generous?"

***

Damn it, damn it, damn it.

I pushed myself away from my desk at Guilty Pleasures, not caring that my chair slammed into the file cabinet when I stood. Stomping to the door of the kitchen, I glanced around until I spotted Roderick, who was standing at one of the metal prep tables meticulously shaving a block of chocolate into the curls we sold and used as garnishes.

"What's up boss lady?" He asked, looking up from his work with a smile.

"*Please* tell me you know things about... computers and technology and things."

"Depends on what you need."

I sighed, gently banging the side of my head in the door-frame. "The inventory program, it will not update for me, and I have been trying for nearly an hour."

Roderick grimaced. "*That*, I can't help with. Do you want me to call Carter? I'm sure he can—"

"No. No, it's fine. It's the middle of the day, he probably has clients at the shop."

"Nah," Rod said, shaking his head. "Carter barely goes to the shop anymore, he's been making plans for his tech business. His college homeboy Brandon put him in touch with some chick from Texas who needs help building a program to help her organize some fancy speed dating shit for old single people."

I lifted an eyebrow. "Old single people?"

"Yeah. Like, in their thirt—.... um, never mind. You want me to call him?"

"No," I said, scowling at him for his "old people" crack. "I will see if I can figure it out."

Since Eddie showed me that video of Carter basically spilling out his heart, I had been... not *exactly* avoiding him, but I certainly hadn't put myself in a position for conversation either. Two days had passed, and truthfully, my emotions were in disarray when it came to him. There was a little voice over one shoulder frantically screaming that I should go to him, embrace him, explain to him that now, I "got" it, and I was willing to offer my heart again now that I understood where he was. However, the voice over the *other* shoulder was composed, and calm. *It* was saying... what if you go to him and he is still not ready? What if you put yourself out there — for *him*— yet again, only for it to get stomped on? Could *I* accept the emotional load of a man who had so much to say *about* our relationship, or lack thereof, yet nothing to say *to* me?

So, no, I did not want Rod to call his brother, because I wasn't ready to be in the room with Carter. Not yet. But thirty minutes later, I still had *not* figured anything out about the computer, and I was so frustrated over it that I wasn't even annoyed when Carter spoke my name from the doorway of my office. Rod had obviously called him *anyway*.

"Hey... Rod said you were having some computer troubles?"

"Yeah," I nodded. "I cannot get this thing to update my

stock like it should… If you could look at it for me…"

He smiled, sending heat that was now almost *expected* rushing between my thighs. "Of course. Get up, let me see what I can do."

I relinquished my seat at the desk, taking a deep inhale as he passed me to sit down. *Damn* I missed that clean, leathery smell of *him*. His shirt, which I still had, had lost it long ago, and in a brief moment of insanity one day in the laundry room, I considered switching it out for another. When I opened the dryer, they were *all* right there, the Fresh Cuts logos taunting me *"Just take one, Frenchy, he won't miss it."*, before I recognized that those were crazy thoughts, and closed the lid…. but not before putting my head close for a nice, full sniff.

So, as long as I didn't let my thoughts drift to emotional things, it was quite pleasant having Carter in my office, with me sitting on the file cabinet behind the desk so that he was near enough to still smell. "So I heard you have been working on building your software business," I said, choosing what felt like a neutral topic, since I couldn't stand the silence. "I was glad to hear it… I know it was something you wanted to do."

"Yeah," he said, giving me a short glance before he turned back to the screen. "Decided to go ahead and take the plunge."

I nodded. "Very good. And… it seems like you are making great strides with Roderick… he has not been in trouble the entire… what has it been now, two months, that he has been here?"

"He has *not*." There was tangible relief in Carter's response, and it made me smile. "Speaking of Rod, how has he been with you? Has he been doing okay?" He spun the chair around, turning to face me. "I've been wanting to hear it from you, but we were... you know." A note of sadness crossed his face, but he quickly schooled his features into an amiable mask. "Anyway, I kind of assumed the fact that you hadn't dragged him back to me by the ear was a good sign."

"It was," I said, with another affirming nod. "Once I set him straight that first day, after calling me a "cougar", he has been wonderful. He works very hard, learns fast. And he is very sweet. I think he looks at me as kind of a big sister."

Carter cocked his head to the side and lifted an eyebrow, but didn't respond before he turned the chair back around to face the computer.

"Whoa, wait a minute!" I caught the arm of the chair, turning him back to face me. "What is that about?"

"Nothing," he said, barely holding back a grin as he shook his head. "If you think Rod thinks of you as a sister..."

"You think he does not?"

"He's a teenaged kid, Viv! Have you seen yourself in a mirror?"

I scoffed. "I do not think he thinks of me like that anymore, not now that we have been working together, and we have established a relationship."

With his elbow propped on the arm of the chair, he dropped his head into his hand. "Okay Viv. I'm gonna let you hold on to that dream."

"Oh, come on, Carter, stop bluffing. It cannot possibly be—"

"Viv...." He reached forward to grab my hands, clutching them between his. "You know that picture of you, in the caramel?"

"Mmhmm." I tried to ignore the tingle rushing over my skin from the contact with his.

"I had to threaten physical violence on my baby brother, and start locking the door to my bedroom after I went home early one day and caught him ja—"

"No!" I yanked my hands away from his to cover my mouth. "No, no, no, no, no. *No*. Nooo, why would you tell me such a thing?!"

"You didn't believe me, I tried to warn you."

I gave him a playful smack him on the shoulder. "That was a terrible visual to give me about my employee. And won't he be embarrassed about you telling such a story?"

Carter let out a burst of laughter. "*Rod*? Embarrassed? Viv, *no*. He's a teenager, it's just what they do. If he knew I told you that story, it would make his little ass more bold, and he would probably ask you if you wanted to watch. I know this because on *another* occasion, my dumb ass forgot about knocking, and I caught him in his room with his little girlfriend doing exactly that."

"Bria?" I asked, lips parted.

"That's the girl who works the front for you here sometimes?"

"Yes."

"Then, yeah. So... I wanted to bleach my fucking eyes, but I learned my lesson, and made sure to give *him* another lesson about condoms, and all of that."

"Wow."

He gave a half-shrug. "My sentiments exactly. But... I mean, as far as *trouble*... he hasn't been any, other than getting on my nerves."

"I am pretty sure that is standard little brother protocol," I said, laughing.

"Indeed. But... After years of... basically nothing, I'm glad to have him around. Happy to be getting things back into a good place now... Thank you for helping with that."

My eyes went wide. "Me? I have done nothing."

"You've done *plenty*," he said, lifting his hands for emphasis. "I mean... you gave him the job here, you encouraged me to give him a chance. Made me keep an open mind about it. So... thank you." He nodded, then turned back to the computer to finish fixing my problem. Silence lay over us again, and it wasn't uncomfortable, but I still felt the need to continue the conversation. This time seemed to be just as good as any other, so before I could second guess it, I folded my hands in my lap and spoke.

"So... I also heard that you got on stage at Urban Grind."

Carter stiffened, and his hands stilled over the keys. "Um... yeah. I did."

"I was surprised," I continued, when he didn't say anything else. "I would not have expected that."

"Yeah, me either," he said, finally turning to face me. "Rod... I don't know if he told you, but he failed one of the sections on his GED. And I mean... I know he knows the material, he's a smart kid, I think he just got too into his head about it, clammed up. So, I was trying to get him to just step out of his comfort zone, but he said some bullshit about me stepping out of mine first... so here we go."

I lifted an eyebrow, remembering how excited Rod had been just last week — the day before Carter's performance, actually — to come back and tell me that he passed his test. I told Carter so, and he scrubbed a hand over his face, shaking his head as he reclined in the chair. "That little mother-fucker... I'm gonna kick his ass. Why would he...?"

"To get you out of your comfort zone, maybe? I mean... how did you feel afterward?"

He shrugged. "I... I guess it was pretty cathartic."

"Good," I said, giving him a wide smile. "I... wish I had been there."

"Yeah... me too."

Our eyes met, and I swallowed hard, wondering why the words to tell him that I'd seen, that I'd *heard* him wouldn't come forth. Before I could say *anything*, he was up, pushing the chair into the desk. "Well, this is fixed," he said, gesturing toward the computer. "It shouldn't give you anymore trouble. I've actually gotta get to a teleconference with a potential client, so... I have to go."

I nodded, suddenly feeling awkward and nervous as he stood in front of me. "Yeah. Yeah, thank you so much. I didn't mean to take up so much of your time with this."

"It's nothing, Viv. You can call me for help with anything. Anytime." The embrace he pulled me into caught me off guard. It was casual, but tight enough that I felt the warm security I remembered from before, from all the nights I'd spent wrapped in his arms. And then it was over, way too quickly for me to be satisfied, and he was striding out of my office into the kitchen.

"Yo, Rod. Come 'ere for a second, man. Let me talk to you."

"What's up man? Did you get it fi— *ouch*. What the fuck, bruh?"

"Oh... I'm sorry. Did I accidentally hit you?"

chapter
eleven

Vivienne

I HATED THIS TIME OF YEAR. AUTUMN I COULD handle, because who doesn't like cute boots and scarves? But *Winter...* ugh. With the snow, and cold winds, and darkness coming earlier in the day. My apartment was already pitch black by the time I got home in the evenings, and today was no exception. I flipped on my lights, and my eyes fell immediately on...

Damnit! This plant!

I was really going to have to send this thing back to a good home with Simone, because for the life of me, I couldn't manage to get this thing enough sun. I re-buttoned my coat, picked the plant up, and headed up to the roof, hoping those artificial sun lamps were still there.

The roof was covered in a light layer of freshly-fallen snow, but the lamps were still out, to my delight. I flipped one on, and sat my plant down, then straightened up. Glancing across the roof, I saw him, perched on the edge of a bench in the covered outdoor seating area. He wasn't facing me, but I recognized those locs and broad shoulders anywhere. Carter didn't look up as I approached. He just kept staring out over the neighborhood, bathed in the harsh safety light of the roof. When I was beside him, he finally looked up, and I almost wished he hadn't.

Déjà vu.

Only worse. His eyes were red and wet, defined underneath by dark circles. His shoulders were drooped, and it seemed like it sapped a great deal of energy to produce the grimace of a smile he gave when he realized it was me.

I sat down beside him, cupping his face in my hands. "Carter...what's going on?"

"Rod."

Immediately, tightness gripped my chest. "What? Is he..."

"He's fine," Carter said, shaking his head. "He was out with Bria this afternoon, slipped on some ice and hit his damned head on the curb. And... he's gonna be *fine*, so I'm glad for that... but they didn't think so at first. Bria called me crying, talking about his head was open, and blood, and ... that *fucked me up*. But... he's fine. He's gonna be fine. I'm just... seeing him in that hospital bed, after everything with my dad..."

"You are feeling a little distraught?"

He looked up, meeting my eyes. "Yeah. I am. Our mom is there now, and only one person could stay, so... she sent me home. I'd been there for almost seven hours, and she knows about the whole... hospital thing. So... she said I should go home and try to get some sleep. But... I *can't*. So, I'm up here, in the cold, like a lunatic."

"You are *not* a lunatic. You are just... human," I said,

smiling as I cupped his face again. He closed his eyes as he nuzzled his chin into my hands. "Did you forget you had a key?"

He stilled, then looked up at me once more, narrowing his eyes in confusion. "What?"

"I told you I was giving you that key to my apartment for when you couldn't sleep. You never returned it. So... you could have used your key, Carter."

For a long moment, he didn't say anything, but bit his lip as he pushed a handful of hair from my face, then left his fingers buried there at my nape. "Are you telling me... that my key still works?"

I smiled, blinking profusely in an attempt to fight back tears. "Always."

Carter

Well... this was unexpected.

The *very* last place I thought I would end up after leaving the hospital was Viv's bed. It certainly wasn't planned, but here I was... I was just grateful to have her in my arms again. She looked so damned peaceful, still asleep, lips parted, her head tucked under my arm as her chest rose and fell. I knew I missed her, but I didn't realize it would feel like *this*, like I couldn't make my heart stop racing, couldn't quite catch my breath. I barely even wanted to sleep myself, but exhaustion won.

We had only talked a little, but that was okay for now. After she told me my key would *always* work — which, by the way... *whew* — we left the roof and went to her apartment. She sent me to the shower, and must have run out while I was in the bathroom, because when I went back into her kitchen, there was a styrofoam plate from the burger spot on the corner waiting for me.

"Feel better?" Viv asked, her eyes drifting conspicuously over my chest, stomach, then down to the towel wrapped around my waist. She bit her lip, and my mouth went dry.

"Yeah. I do. Thanks." I sat down at the counter, trying to ignore the almost compulsive need to touch her. If I did, right now, while she was looking at me like *that*, I was going to turn this reunion into something else entirely.

Viv finally dragged her eyes back up to my face, and smiled. "Good. I already ate, so I'm gonna go take a shower myself, then go to bed.... okay?" She didn't look away until I nodded, confirming that I'd caught what she meant.

Thirty minutes later, I was stretched on "my" side of her bed, close to drifting off as I wondered what was taking her so long. I was barely keeping my eyes open, hypnotized by the projection of stars onto the ceiling from the new night-light plugged into the wall when she finally emerged from the bathroom.

"When did you get this?" I asked, lazily pointing to sky, my voice thick with sleepiness.

I heard one of her drawers slide open. "A few weeks ago. My cousin's stepdaughter was selling them for school fundraising."

"Cool. What took you so long in the bathroom?" I sat up, resting my back against her headboard as she entered the bed from the other side, sitting up on her knees. With her hair pulled up in a high ponytail, fresh-faced, in just a tee shirt — regrettably, not one of mine — she was... gorgeous.

Always, *always* gorgeous. The only light in the room came from the projection of those stars, creating tiny pinpricks of light over her skin.

"Why so many questions?"

"Why so few answers?"

She grinned, then pushed herself to shimmy a little closer to me across the bed. "Well... since I was not being... *intimate* with anyone, I may or may not have taken a little hiatus from shaving my legs. It was time to resume."

"So what you're saying is you were in there clogging up your bathtub drain."

Laughing, Viv scooted forward again until her knees were against my thigh. I didn't want to assume anything, so while she was in the shower, I'd run back to my place for fresh boxers and a pair of sweats. Still, the heat from her body carried through, and this time, I didn't resist the urge to reach out, sliding my hand from her ankle, over her calf, and up to rest behind her knee.

Viv was holding her breath. From the moment I touched her, air hitched in her threat, and she didn't release it until I dragged my hand further up, to her thigh, stopping just before I hit gold. Without a word, she swung her leg over my lap so that she was straddling me. She draped her hands over my shoulders, then lowered her forehead to mine as her soft hands slipped inside my boxers to pull me free. For what seemed like a long time, we stayed like that, just staring, and Viv's eyes... they were saying a lot.

She was anxious, and excited, and turned on, and uncertain, and scared, and... hopeful. I brought my hands up to cup her face, and she seemed to melt into my touch, her shoulders sagging in relief. But then, a tear ran from the corner of her eye, sliding down her face. "Viv... what is it?"

"You hurt me." Those words burst out like they'd been struggling to break free for a long time. "*So* bad, Carter. I thought you were going to be different... you *were* different, until... until you were exactly the same as the others. I have spent so much time trying not to lo—" she stopped herself with a dry laugh before shaking her head to continue, "Trying not to care so much for you. But it seems that I cannot. So... I need to *know*, Carter. I do not want to be fool-ish. I do *not* want to keep making this same mistake. I can't keep giving myself to you, if you can't... I need to know that I am not in this alone."

I lifted her chin to face me. "You're not. You're *not*."

She turned away, focusing on one of the illuminated shapes on the wall. "But you said you did not —"

Shit.

"I know," I said, turning her to me again. "I *know*. I fucked up, I'll own that. I said it." Again, she tried to break away, but I cupped her face, keeping her focused on me so I could meet her gaze. "I told you I didn't ask you for your heart, but I *never* said that I didn't want it. I *need* it. And I need *you*. Okay?"

Please say okay.

I hoped it was enough. Hoped she understood that even *those* words were hard for me to say. I felt... wide open, exposed... fucking vulnerable beyond belief, somehow even more than I had that night when I put my entire ego on the line. Why was it that with her, the person that made me feel *so* damned alive... when it came to telling her how I felt, all of that energy turned into cold, paralyzing fear that *"dude... you're not good enough for this beautiful girl if your own—"*

"Okay."

A shot of adrenaline, right into the chest.

That's how that one little word felt to me, and I was suddenly *very* awake as Viv kissed me. Or maybe *attacked* was a better word, but I was a willing victim as teeth clacked, lips bruised, tongues clashed in a reunion that had taken two months too long to happen. I was a happy man, thanking my lucky stars for this moment when she accidentally nipped my bottom lip too hard. I flinched a little, pulling away for a second to see if blood would follow, but I really wasn't tripping.

Viv, on the other hand, freaked out. She apologized profusely as she reached over to turn on the lamp so she could see. She had *not* drawn blood, but it wasn't until I gently grabbed her face again, forcing her to look at me as I carefully stated "It's okay" that she relaxed, and reached for the lamp again.

"Uh-uh," I said. "Leave it on. I haven't seen you. I wanna *see* you."

Her eyes glossy, and still slightly red from her earlier tears, she reached for the hem of her shirt and pulled it over her head. Just like always, my hands went immediately to her breasts, running my thumbs over her chosen jewelry for the night— simple, pretty hoops in rose gold.

"I am starting to think you are obsessed," Viv said, smiling as I lowered my mouth to kiss her nipples.

"Maybe a little."

She moaned her appreciation when I pulled one into my mouth, suckling until she was writhing in my lap. I'd already peeped out that she was panty-less under her tee shirt, but when my hand drifted there, she pushed me away. She raised up on her knees, grabbed me, and was about to maneuver herself down when I caught her by the thighs.

"Are you crazy? After two months, you think I'm not about to take my time with you?"

Viv smirked, then started stroking me with her hands as she gave me a long, deep kiss, the dual sensations damn near making my toes curl — in the manliest way possible. "Carter... *I* think I need to feel you like *this* now... the other stuff can wait until later."

Who was I to argue with *that*? I released her thighs, and she sank down onto me with a satisfied sigh. Just like that, I was invited back into heaven.

We made love until we were too exhausted to move, then passed out, and I woke up the next morning with her clutched in my arms. I fumbled blindly, eyes still shut, averse to giving up on sleep, for my phone on the table next to her bed. Its' buzzing was what woke me up, and when my hand landed on it, I grudgingly opened my eyes to look at the screen. The sight of a missed call from my mom, and a text from Rod asking where I was brought me fully awake. I extricated myself from Viv's embrace and took another shower, then went back to kiss her forehead.

"Hey... I've gotta go see about Rod, okay?" I said, when she finally opened her eyes.

She narrowed them, giving me a few confused blinks before her circuits started firing. "Oh. *Oh*! Do you want me to come with you?" She brought her hand to my face, concern filling her eyes.

"No, I've got it. Go back to sleep, it's like five in the

morning," I said, reluctantly pulling the discarded sheets up to cover her beautifully nude body. I kissed her hand, then stood, groaning when she sat up, causing the sheet to drop away again.

It was insane how oblivious she was to her overt sex appeal, and I knew this wasn't an "act" for Viv, something she did just to try and seduce me. She had *that* effect whether she was trying or not. This was just... *her*, and had always been, from the moment I first spoke to her.

"Carter?"

"Yeah?" I asked, clearing my throat.

Following my gaze to her breasts, she blushed, then pulled the covers over herself. "I was *saying* that I want you to be careful out there in the snow. I do not want to get the same kind of call you got about Rod."

"Okay mama hen," I teased, giving her a peck on the lips that quickly turned into me pressing her onto the bed to ease my tongue into her mouth.

She indulged me for a few minutes, then pushed me away. "You have to go."

"I know."

"And when you return... we have to talk."

I nodded. "I know."

She lifted her hand to my face. "And... you *will* return?"

"Of course."

***

"*Goddamn*, Rod! Have they let you see your *face*?"

That was the first thing I said to Roderick when I walked into his room at the hospital. His eyes bulged. "What the fuck are you talking about, man? Gimme a mirror or something!"

"I don't have one," I shrugged. "But your shit is *messed* up."

I fought hard not to laugh as he glanced around frantically for something he could use to see his reflection. "Dude, where the fuck is my phone?!"

"Rod, *relax*, man. Nothing's wrong with your face, pretty boy. How you managed to knock your own damned head in, but *not* mess up your face, I don't understand."

"Cause I'm the handsome brother, Carter. Ugly dudes like you don't have those sort of problems."

I laughed as I approached the bed to fist bump Rod. "I see a mild concussion doesn't keep you from talking shit."

"*Nothing* will keep me from talking shit. Where you been, man?" He asked as I took a seat in the empty chair beside the bed. "When I saw Mom here but not you... I thought you had maybe bailed on me."

Rod had his eyes trained on me, intense as he waited for my response. I slid to the edge of the chair, reaching out to bump his fist again. "I told you this shit already man. Never again."

When our gazes met, he nodded, then seemed to relax. "So... you didn't say where you were, so you must have gotten caught up with something. Or *somebody*." He grinned as he wiggled his eyebrows, then cringed when his movements aggravated the laceration on his head.

"That's what you get for being in grown folks business," I ragged him. "Where did Mom and Bria go? I didn't see them in the hall."

"Breakfast. Yo, Moms actually likes Bria. It's blowing my mind."

I chuckled. "What, you're gonna dump her now since the parents approve?"

Rod turned up his lip, scowling at me like I'd said something outrageous. "Man, hell nah. Bria is fly. And not *just* fly, like the chicks my age back home. She's like... smart and shit too."

"So you came up here and fell in puppy love with a city girl," I teased, reclining against the back of my chair.

He grinned. "Just like my brother."

I shrugged it off with a smile, but the thought of that made me feel like somebody had turned the heat up a little too high. He was right, obviously, but it was a little unnerving that he could see that about me. "I don't know what you're talking about man."

"Okay," he said, sucking his teeth. "So that five million word essay you read about Viv at Urban Grind was just for fun, right?"

I cocked an eyebrow. "You must be forgetting I still owe you an ass-whipping for the shit you pulled, lying to get me up on stage that night."

"You should be thanking me. You put it all out there on the table now."

"To everybody except *her*, genius."

He gave me a sheepish smile. "I *did* invite her, just couldn't get her to take me up on it. My heart was in the right place, that's what matters.

I snorted with laughter, and was about to respond when the door swung open, revealing my mom and Bria on the other side. Rod lost interest in me as Bria rushed up to the bed. Smiling wide, my mother grabbed me by the arm and led me out of the room.

"Let's let them have their privacy," she said, leading me to an empty, quiet corner of the waiting room just outside.

Sitting alone with my mom, I didn't really feel any of the things one would expect. I loved her, obviously, because she was my mom, but this felt more like sitting down to catch up with a neighbor who had watched me grow up than the kind of warm familiarity that should exist between mother and son. That... was gone.

"So tell me what's going on with you, son." She was smiling *so* big, looking *so* excited, like this — admittedly rare — occurrence of me and her alone was just making her day.

I shrugged. "Not much."

A flash of hurt crossed her face at my short answer, and inwardly, I cringed. I really wasn't trying to be rude to her, didn't want to make her feel bad. She pulled a smile to her face anyway. "Well, you're looking good, at least. I bet you have all kinds of women after you, a handsome man like you."

I tried to force a grin, but the muscles in my face wouldn't cooperate for anything more than a grimace. "Um... I guess."

She perked up a little, raising an eyebrow at me. "*Ohh.* Must be just one then. The pretty chocolatier Rod has been telling me about, maybe?" She gave me an encouraging nod, but it seemed like my brain shut down further, like it was locking down, protecting my thoughts about Viv.

I gave a half shrug in response, and the smile slid from my mother's face, replaced by a look of dejection.

"Carter... son, can you at least meet me a *quarter* of the way? I'm *trying* here, and you won't even budge."

I snorted. "Yeah, I've noticed that *now* you try."

"What is that supposed to mean? "Now" I try."

"Mom... don't do this, okay? I don't feel like having this conversation right now."

She huffed, sitting back in her chair. "Of course you don't. You get *that* from your father, wanting to shut down and push back the moment the conversation gets tough."

"Don't talk about my dad like that. At least he was there, but you don't know anything about that, do you?" I sucked my teeth, shaking my head as I stood to leave. I wasn't about to do this shit, not here in a suffocating hospital, where I didn't even want to be.

"You sit your butt down, young man," my mother said, raising her voice.

My face turned up in a scowl, but... that was still my mom. I didn't look at her as I sat back down.

"You don't throw a jab like that and walk away from me, Carter. That's not how you solve things. If you've got something you need to say — and you obviously do, you're obviously angry, can barely even look at me — then let's talk about it."

I turned my eyes up toward the ceiling as I shook my head. "Oh, you wanna talk about it," I muttered.

"Yes, I do, actually. We're adults, Carter. Let's talk about it."

"Okay," I said, nostrils flaring as I sat up, resting my elbows on my knees. "Let's talk about how for 18 damned *years* Mom, I only ever heard from you once a week, and saw Christmas come around more times than I saw *you*. Can we talk about that? Can we talk about how as soon as Rod turns 16 and starts acting a clown, all of a sudden you're calling me two, three times a week, pretending like you gave a shit about what was happening with me, when you really just needed me to try to talk some sense into him. Let's talk about how since Rod has been up here with me, your ass has been on a plane damn near weekly to see him. Come on, mom. *Talk*."

For a long time, she just stared at me, eyes glossy with tears before she nodded. "Okay." She cleared her throat, then nodded again. "We can talk about how I only called once a week, because that's how long it took me to gather up enough strength to spend that hour talking to you without having a breakdown over the phone. We can absolutely discuss that every time I came to see you, knowing that I couldn't take you home, it *killed* me, so I took the coward's way out, and stayed away. And yes, once Rod started getting in trouble, I did turn to you because his dad was gone. He needed a strong male bond with someone, and I didn't want to lose him, have him resent me... like you. And we can certainly talk about how my visits up here have *not* been just to see your brother. I wanted to see *you* too."

I scoffed. "So that's it, huh? You have all your answers wrapped up in a neat little box for me, ready to go."

"Oh it's not neat at all, son. It's *messy*. It's very, very messy, but you left to be with your father when you were ten years old, Carter. I've had twenty years to figure out how to put it concisely."

"*Left to be with my fa—* do you even *hear* yourself? Left to be with my father, like it was some extended sleepover. Nah, mom. *You* abandoned me," I said, struggling to keep my voice down as heat built in my chest.

Her eyes went wide. "Abandoned, Carter? Do you think I had a choice? I got *arrested*. Because I was driving home tipsy from work and smacked my car into a mailbox. I spent the night in jail, *praying* that you were okay because I was in too much of a damned slump to even remember a phone number to call somebody to go see about you, and I was terrified to tell the police you were home by yourself, because I knew they would take you. And guess what? When I finally broke down and said something because they were about to keep me another day, they did exactly that. Carter it broke my heart for that social worker to come and tell me *you* were being detained for fighting the officers that came to the apartment, telling them you couldn't go anywhere cause you were waiting for your mom. I made a *mess.*"

"But they didn't keep me," I said, shaking my head to clear away *that* memory. "Mrs. White, the lady from the apartment next door told them I was staying with her, and she was just letting me go back to sleep in my own bed at night. They let me go, and you had a chance once you got out, but you still didn't fight."

She gave a dry laugh. "With what strength, Carter? Fight with what? When your father found out about that, he wanted you with him, and what could I do to stop him? I was a drunk, and on depression medicines for a chemical imbalance that left me like a zombie half the time. What kind of life was I giving you?"

"We were good, mom," I insisted, swallowing the lump in my throat. You *were* taking care of me, and when you couldn't I took care of you. We... we were a *team*. That's what you said."

She shook her head, clapping a hand over her mouth to

choke back a sob. "*No*, baby. That wasn't healthy, son. You were a little boy, not a man, not yet."

"But I did the best I could."

"You did, baby," she nodded. "You absolutely did. You cooked for me, and you had your little paper route, you... you were the *best* son a mommy could want, Carter, but it doesn't change the fact that it wasn't okay for you to feel like you *had* to take care of me. That wasn't your job, Carter. I had it in my head that I would fight for you, that I would fight for custody, but every time I thought about you getting pulled outta that apartment by the police.... you needed to be with your dad, and I needed to clean myself up."

I scowled, ignoring the headache that was brewing from me clenching my jaw. "Yeah, you did that, and then still didn't come back for me, since you had your new husband, and your new kid. No need to go back for the one that's already fucked up, right?"

She cocked her head to the side, then stood, coming to sit on the table in front of me. "*Wrong*," she said, cupping my face in her hands. I tried to pull away, but she held tight, forcing me to look at her. "Son, I think you're forgetting the way those early conversations went. The tears over the phone, the tantrums, acting out. There was already so much damage done. Your father and stepmother insisted on no more than once a week, and pushed for less than that, but I wouldn't let them take *that* away. I wasn't even supposed to call on your birthday, because they didn't want you to get all upset. Those conversations were just as hard on you as they were on me, and I felt you drifting away. You were growing up. And once you got old enough to decide if you wanted to talk to me or not... you chose *not*. And I don't blame you, so

I didn't push. By that point, I was just some lady you had to talk to. Your father and Denise were your parents by then, and you were thriving."

"They didn't even "get" me though. Yeah, they took good care of me, but I needed the person who understood that I'd rather figure out how to make a robot throw a football than learn how to do it myself. I *needed* you. I was *angry*, Mom. And I was hurt because the one person who "got" me, didn't want me. It still feels fucked up *now*. Do you have any idea how fucked up it is to feel like that when you're a *kid*?"

She nodded, then pulled me into an embrace. To my own surprise, I didn't resist. "I can imagine, sweetheart," she said, clutching me tight against her. "I am *so*, so sorry."

Being this close to her was awkward at first, but after a moment, I gave in to the urge to return her embrace. She stiffened in surprised, then burst into noisy tears, and before long, my eyes were burning too. My mother looked up, chin trembling as she tried to smile. She gave a heavy sigh, then brought her hand to my face.

"Carter, I don't expect to heal twenty years of hurt in a single conversation. I understand this isn't Iyanla," she said, then laughed at her joke. "But... baby, I want you to know, it was not Mommy's intention to abandon you. Depression is a *very* dark place Carter, that I couldn't get out of on my own, not without *major* help. I still struggle sometimes, to this day. Your assessment that I "replaced" you and your father... honestly, it's fair." She nodded as her eyes welled with fresh tears. "I think I was trying to have a do-over. Fix what I didn't get right the first time, and it was absolutely not fair to you. Not at all, Carter. But I need you to understand that it was *not* because I somehow loved Roderick more than you.

There was so much damage done already that I really thought it was better to leave you be."

I shook my head. "You thought wrong, mom. I was praying that I would see you show some effort, and it didn't seem like that happened until you wanted me to step in for you with Rod. But I guess that's what happens when you wait twenty years to have a conversation."

"It wasn't *your* responsibility. It was mine. It was the other adults'. *We* should have behaved better, and maybe things would be different now. I think about the things your stepmother used to say to me, and... whew. I could still choke her now."

"Why does she hate you so much?" I asked, sitting back. "She never bad-mouthed you to me, but I'd be lying if I said I never overheard her with dad."

My mother huffed. "And I'm sure that didn't exactly help my reputation with you."

I grimaced. "Probably not."

"Not surprised," she said, laughing. "Your stepmother's problem with me is that your father still wanted me. Once I was cleaned up, he was always making little innuendos over the phone before he handed it off to you, and that burned her up... so obviously she channeled that anger into being mad at *me*, instead of her husband."

"But that was a lot of years ago. She's still mad?"

My mother smirked. "Oh, honey... no. She's still mad at the fact that about a year before he got sick, your daddy packed up his bags and showed up at my door talking about he was back for me. Was gonna help me raise your brother, since *his* father had already passed at that time."

"Are you serious?" I asked, eyes wide.

She nodded. "Very much so. And I sent his ass packing, back on whatever train he rolled in on. Your father was a good daddy, I'll give him that. But he never took my depression seriously, that's why he let you stay with me. He swore it was just "womanly" moods, since it happened suddenly. It wasn't triggered by any certain event, it just... *was.* But your father... he insisted that I was just being mean to him, didn't want him around. I passed on his offer to "start anew", and sent him back home to his wife. *That's* what she's so salty about."

"Wow," I said, chuckling as I shook my head.

She smiled. "So I *can* still make you laugh, huh?" She placed her hand over mine on my knee. "Carter... again, I know this doesn't really fix anything, but I'm glad we got this out. I hope you feel the same."

"I do... I... I guess I actually do feel better."

"Good," she said, squeezing my hand. "You think you can talk to me now? Like we used to? Remember, it wasn't always bad, right? You had fun on the phone with me sometimes."

That was true. My mom was the one who asked about the things I really cared about. Business, and programming, and anime, and all the shit I got teased for while living with my dad, so I pretended to be a jock instead. She kept saying she didn't think this conversation was supposed to fix anything, but truthfully, I kinda felt like a burden was lifted. Seeing my mom cry over this, hearing her talk about it with emotion that couldn't be faked... having her tell me that she never meant to disregard me... I *needed* that, had been needing it for twenty years.

And she looked *so* happy.

"Yeah, mom. We can talk." I was able to give her a real smile that time, and she returned it with a grin of her own.

"Okay... so let's talk about the French girl. Roderick said something about her being covered in caramel, and I'm not sure—"

"*Come on,* Mom."

chapter
twelve
Carter

I DIDN'T GO BACK TO VIV IMMEDIATELY.

Once I left the hospital, after spending the next few hours with Rod, my mom, and Bria, I went back up to my usual spot on the roof of our building to clear my head, and process everything. The talk with my mother, the reunion with Viv, the restored relationship with Rod... everything was lining up a little too neatly.

But that's that defeatist attitude again, man.

... Right. And I was sick of that holding me in the same place. I thought back to the conversation with Roman — what had he said? Something about doing something different if I wanted a different result, and that had to apply to my thoughts too, right? If shit falling apart was what I always expected, that's what was bound to happen. So maybe a little bit of just happily going with the flow was in order.

The sun was heading down, and I glanced across the roof as I stood, noticing that Viv's plant was still there from last night. It didn't look to be in the best of shape after sitting in the cold overnight, but the heat from the solar powered artificial sun lamp had helped. I turned off the lamp, sending up a silent thank you to God that I'd gotten to it before the energy conservation nuts in our building had, and picked up the plant.

A couple of minutes later, I was in front of Viv's door, raising my hand to knock. Before I could make contact, her door swung open, and there she was, dressed to head out in the cold. She startled, seeming almost surprised to see me. Her eyes went wide, and were red, like she'd been crying.

"Hey...," I said, wracking my mind to try to figure out what was going on with her.

She swallowed, focusing her gaze on the plant before giving me a little half smile. "Hey yourself."

"Where you heading?"

"To get something to eat. Craving pancakes."

I grinned, trying to break whatever the awkward tension between us. "If you have the ingredients... I can make you some."

For some reason, her shoulders seemed to sag in relief, and she gave me a grateful smile. "I think I might."

"Well... what are we waiting for, come on."

Stepping past her into the apartment, I put the plant in its usual spot by the window, then took off my coat and hung it up. Viv had closed the front door, but was still standing by it, so I tugged her out of her coat too. "What's wrong with you?" I asked, pulling her into the kitchen so I could start taking down ingredients.

"Nothing." Viv shook her head and smiled, but her tone was unconvincing. Leaning against the counter, she took a deep breath, then said, "So... turned into a busy day for you?" She was trying to sound casual, but her words held an edge of desperation that made my heart clench.

I turned to her, and the note of fear in her eyes confirmed my suspicion. "You thought I wasn't coming back..."

Immediately, her eyes welled up as she nodded. "It's completely psycho, I know. I just... I texted you a few times today, and I called, and I haven't heard from you, and it just... it reminded me so much of that first day that Darren disappeared before he came back *engaged*, and I just... I guess I just convinced myself of the worst."

"Viv..." I reached for her, pulling her close against my chest for a moment before I picked her up, placing her on the edge of the counter. I stood between her legs, tipping up her chin so her teary gaze could meet mine. "That shit isn't happening, okay? Not here. I... I got scared. That's just what happened. And I fucked up, for *so* many reasons. But... I've gotta put that shit to the side. I know it's hard to trust that when I haven't been open with you, baby, but *believe me...* I'm *trying*."

She nodded, pulling her top lip between her teeth. "I know." She lifted her hands, running them through my locs before burying her fingers at the base of my neck. "I saw you... that night at Urban Grind. Eddie filmed it with his phone, and showed me the video. So... I know."

A heavy feeling dropped into my stomach, and for a fleeting moment, I wanted to pull away and withdraw, knowing that she'd heard everything. Like... *everything*. All of the fears, all of the insecurities, everything I worked *damn* hard not to show. But the tears in her eyes held me in place. I *couldn't* do that to her, so instead... I looked at the bright side.

I mimicked the way she was holding on to me, burrowing my fingers into her hair too as I looked her in the eyes. "Then... you should know that I love you, right?" Several tears escaped as she nodded, and I wiped them away with my thumbs. "And... you know that it's not just some shit I'm saying, right? I *for real* love you. No faking, no hiding. You understand that, right?"

Without giving her a chance to respond, I kissed her, hoping that if my words weren't convincing her, this would. I poured everything into it, and when we finally pulled back, out of breath and panting, she nodded again. "I love you too."

I smiled, then propped my forehead against hers, feeling suddenly drained. "Your hair is damp," I said, breaking the silence that had fallen between us. "You were going out in the cold with damp hair?" I pulled back, then slowly unzipped her knee-length boots and pulled them from her feet.

"I just took a shower. Am I in trouble?" she grinned, wiping the last of the tears from her eyes as I reached under her thick sweater dress to pull her leggings and panties from her waist. She lifted her hips so I could get them over her legs.

Smirking, I tossed the clothes to the floor and stepped between her legs. "Would you like to be?"

She bit her lip as I slid my fingers inside her, and scooted closer to the edge, inviting me in deeper. "Maybe." With handfuls of my locs clutched in her fingers, she tugged me down to kiss me as she rocked her hips against my hand.

"You sure you don't wanna stop to eat? You seemed pretty hungry."

"No," she said, then leaned back on her hands, spreading her legs wider. "*You* can eat though."

A slow smile spread over my face as I caught her meaning. "Oh, I can, huh? Right here in the kitchen?"

"Is that not what kitchens are for?" she asked innocently, eyes wide, as she sat up, running her hands over the bulge in the front of my jeans. She made quick work of freeing me from my pants, and then I was in her hands, painfully hard as she dipped her fingers in her own wetness, then used that to begin stroking me. "Perhaps... I can find us a little chocolate?"

"As good as that sounds, I just wanna be inside you right now."

With one hand still wrapped around me, Viv draped the other arm over my shoulder and leaned forward to whisper into my ear. "What are you waiting for?"

Not a damned thing. She guided me inside of her, moaning as I burrowed as far as I could. I yanked her dress over her head, and that went on the floor too after I kicked my way out of my shoes and pants without removing myself from her body. She leaned back on her hands again as I pulled off my own shirt, then lifted her legs to wrap around my hips.

She stayed like that, with her lip between her teeth, breasts bouncing, watching as I disappeared into her over and over again. "Goddamn, Frenchy. Do you have *any* idea how fucking beautiful you look like this?"

"Call me that again," she said in a throaty whisper, looking up at me through half-lidded eyes.

"Beautiful?"

She shook her head, then draped an arm around my neck to pull her herself up, so her chest was flush against mine. "No." Her eyes were glossy again, and for a moment I was near-panicked, wondering what I had said or done. She gave me a soft, lingering kiss, then said, "Say my name again."

"*Oh.*" I grinned, pulling her closer as she ground her hips against mine. "I love you, Frenchy."

She smiled. "I love you too, Carter."

Vivienne

Questions. I had so, so many questions for Carter, but the last thing I wanted to do was overwhelm him, right after he'd just given me *so* much. He told me he loved me, and then he made love *to* me, and then he made me those pancakes he'd promised. Now, we were in my bed, and Carter's head was resting on my chest. Neither of us had said anything for a long while, and I thought maybe he was asleep, but then he spoke.

"I talked to my mom today," he said, lifting his head to look at me. "While I was at the hospital." I nodded, but said nothing, and he lifted an eyebrow. "That's a big deal, Frenchy."

Again, I nodded. "I'm glad. I'm happy for you... I think?"

"You think?" he asked, lifting an eyebrow.

I gave him a little smile. "Carter... I do not really know the story, so I don't know if you talking to your mother is a good thing or not. I'm hoping that it *is*?"

He dropped his head. "Yeah... it is."

"I am sorry," I said, running my hands through his locs. "I did not mean to ruin your news. I just... I did not want to have the wrong reaction, since I do not know—"

"*Viv*," he lifted his head again, then pulled himself up so that we were at eye level with each other. "*I'm* sorry. It's not like you can know something I haven't shared with you... right?"

"Right." I brought my hand up to cup his face. "I know that it is hard for you to open up, but I want you to know that you *can* with me. I want to know you, Carter. The *real* Carter."

He scoffed. "Come on, Viv. You do know me."

"Uh-uh. I know the Carter on the exterior. I want to know the *real* Carter. I want to know your stories, and your frustrations, and the things that you don't want anybody else to know. I want to know the scared little boy you talked about in your poem, and the scared grown man you talked about too. I already know *this*," — I waved my hand over him — "Carter. I want to know *this,*" — I placed my hand over his heart — "Carter. The one you keep tucked away for no one else to see. You are *safe* with me. I promise."

He smiled, taking my face in his hands to pull me into a kiss. "I know."

"Good. And don't you *ever* forget."

"I won't," he chuckled.

Then, he pulled me into his arms, keeping me pressed close as he told me about the talk with his mom, which led into a full-blown history of their past. He talked about tense moments growing up with a father who didn't understand him — something I could certainly relate to, and made me cry explaining why celebrating my birthday was so important to him — because he knew how it felt to be overlooked by your parents on that day.

Slowly, I realized the truth in Simone's words, that Carter wasn't who he appeared to be at all. The more I learned, the more layers he dug up for me... the more I fell in love. And it wasn't *pity* for him, not at all. Yes, he'd had a hard road as a child, but it was the fact that even though this was *hard* for him, even though these memories hurt... he was baring his soul to me, because he recognized that I needed it. He was putting his entire self on the line to regain my trust, and my heart was so full I thought it might burst.

"You don't have to do this," I said, placing my fingers over his lips to stop him. "Not all at once, not right now."

"Are you sure? Because—"

"Yes, Carter. I am sure. I... I understand. You don't have to drain yourself like this, not for me. If it is helpful for you, by all means, continue, but... I just want you to know you can be open with me. "

He nodded, then laid back on the bed with a tired, heavy sigh. "I know. And... I can, but damn... this shit is draining, you know? And a lot easier said than done."

"Of course. It always is. Kind of like not falling for someone who only wants to be your friend," I teased. "You know... you said some really beautiful things about me in that poem." I turned onto my stomach, positioning myself close enough to plant a kiss against his lips.

He buried his hand in my hair, keeping me pulled close. "I *feel* some really beautiful things *for* you."

"The feeling is mutual... but unintended."

"Yeah, I didn't mean to love you either, Frenchy. But I do," he said, kissing the faint scar on my forehead from a night that seemed like a lifetime ago. Being with him like this... this incredibly simple moment ... *this* was love. Not the unwitting infatuation of a young girl with a man old enough to be her father, or the desperate contentment of a defeated woman with a man who barely even made her smile. *This*, me and Carter, sharing kisses that still tasted like pancakes... this was it.

"I love you too."

Carter

It felt like second nature this time.

There was no worry, no doubts, as Viv and I ventured forward, together. *For real* together. As in, she was mine. *Mine*. And that wasn't on any possessive, she had to do what I said type of shit, but knowing that I had her heart — and she gave it willingly, *generously* — man, it worked wonders for being able to offer her the same. When we were together, it just flowed. No awkward moments, no uncomfortable silence, just the kind of easy, organic peace that came from being with somebody you loved, who loved you in return.

It was nothing to go grocery shopping together, for me to sit at her counter working on a program while she tested a recipe, or what we were doing today— visiting Roman and Simone and their new baby— as a couple.

"That's dangerous, man."

I looked up as Roman approached, clapping me on the shoulder as he sat down beside me at his kitchen counter. When I gave him a confused lift of my eyebrow, he inclined his head to where Simone and Viv were sitting in the living room. Viv had their nearly six week old son, Roman Jr. — RJ — cradled in her arms, smiling at him as he looked up at her. Both of their eyes held the same look of wonder, and it made a tightness that wasn't exactly foreign bloom in my chest.

Chuckling, I shook my head. "Yeah... I see what you mean."

"I'm already trying to think of how to talk her into another one, but she said some shit about how she couldn't believe I was asking that when I wasn't even invited back to do the things that *make* a baby yet." He laughed, then turned back to me with a serious expression. "This is... this shit is incredible man, for real. Finding somebody to love, bringing your family to life."

I nodded, but didn't say anything. My eyes were still focused on Viv holding RJ, and it made me wonder what she would look like pregnant with *our* baby, holding *our* baby, loving *our* baby... making up for the mistakes of our own parents.

Later, when we were back in Viv's apartment, making love for the second time that night, I cupped her face as I hovered over her, still buried inside her. "Can we have a baby?"

Her blissful expression shifted to confusion and fear as she met my gaze. "Carter... you cannot be serious. We have been back together for less than two weeks!"

"Not right now," I said soothingly, brushing her hair from her face as I laughed. "I probably should have led with that, I'm sorry. I mean, *later*. *Much* later. I'm asking if you want kids."

She lifted an eyebrow. "You realize that while you are *inside* of me, this is a problematic question to ask, no?"

"I do. I'm sorry." I still couldn't help but chuckle. "You should see your face."

"I can imagine that it is very pissed off," she said, even though she started laughing too. "But... yes. *If* we are able to maintain our love, and *if* we get married... I would love to have children some day."

"Okay. Okay," I nodded. "I just... it's important to me, so..."

"Carter... I understand. I love you."

I smiled, dropping to give her a kiss. "I love you too."

"Now," she said, bringing her hands up to my face. "Can I have my orgasm please?"

***

— 7 months later — — (Roman & Simone's Wedding) —

Viv was still mad at me. If her cursing me out — in French, which somehow made it worse — weren't enough of an indication, the fact that she didn't even look at me, didn't even shoot me a smile as I escorted Simone down the aisle definitely made it clear.

When I sat down, after handing Simone off to Roman, I stared at her until she shifted uncomfortably under my gaze. Finally, she glanced at me.

Got her.

She wasn't *that* mad, couldn't be, not with that smile playing at the corners of her mouth, threatening to break free. She couldn't even stay serious long enough for me to take her seriously, now that I was staring at her, in a way that made it very obvious that I wanted her. *Damn*, I wanted her. I hadn't been with her in a week, after flying to help Rod get settled into his on-campus apartment to start his first semester of college. I'd missed my flight back, and it took a whole day to get another one because of delays, which almost made me late for the wedding. That was the *first* reason she was mad at me.

The second was because as gorgeous as Frenchy looked in her maid of honor gown… she looked a little bit rounder than usual in the middle, and I — idiotically — got a bit overexcited. So, the first thing I did, after not seeing her for a week, was to gently rest my hand against her belly, hoping she could see the unasked question in my eyes.

Short answer — yes. Yes, she did, and my ears were still ringing from the cursing she gave me then, and again thirty minutes later when I called to tell her everything was ready for the bride. She was *pissed*. But now, with all the love in the air between Roman and Simone as they exchanged their vows, she had softened. When I found her in the reception hall after the wedding, she let me pull her into my arms as Jill Scott and Anthony Hamilton sang *So In Love* in the background.

"I should still be mad at you," she said, weaving a little on her feet from one too many glasses of whatever I'd spotted her drinking with Eddie at the open bar. "You called me *fat*."

I chuckled. "I *didn't*. I just… got a little carried away. You know I think you're beautiful, right?"

"Whatever," she said, even though she smiled.

"Seriously… you don't doubt that, right?"

She gave me a slow, deliberate shake of her head. "*No. You can be beautiful and fat.*"

"I know that."

"So I'm noticing that you keep reminding me that I'm beautiful… but no assurance that you don't think I look fat." She raised an eyebrow.

"I *don't*," I insisted, sucking my teeth when she grinned to let me know she was playing. "Your belly was just a little round, so I was hoping... you know."

"I am *bloated* Carter. We are not trying for that, remember? Not until after you and I do *this*," — she gestured around us— , "And who knows when that will be?"

I fought back a grin, thinking about the platinum set diamond ring I'd purchased with my first check from freelance programming, which I planned to give her later that same night, when we were back in our apartment, alone. "Right. But... you mentioned that you were late, so I thought maybe... To be honest, I *hoped* maybe..."

"In due time," she said, smiling. "And to be honest... I may have hoped a little too. But... I got a negative pregnancy test result this morning, and of course my period showed up right after that. The morning of the wedding, of all times." She shook her head, then wrapped her arms around my waist, pressing herself against my chest. "I was a little sad."

"Don't be." I kissed the top of her head as I pulled her tight. "We've got time."

the end

The Serendipitous Love Series:
A Crazy Little Thing Called Love - Roman & Simone
Didn't Mean To Love You - Carter & Viv
Fall In Love Again - Nixon & Charlie
The Way Love Goes - Sean & Fallon
Love You Forever - Sydnee & Harlan
Something Like Love - Eddie & Astrid

To read more from the Heights, visit the <u>Equilibrium Series</u>
next.

Thank you for reading Didn't Mean To Love You.
To continue the series, go straight to <u>Fall In Love Again</u> !

Keep reading for a sneak peak!

one.
charlie.

I *NEVER* CLAIMED TO BE HIS "RIDE OR DIE".

Really, I couldn't understand why he would expect such a thing from me. I mean... it was never a secret — at least not between *us*— that *love* was the very last thing on the list of needs we met for each other. An educated, successful, good-looking, brown-skinned spouse, check, check, check, and *check*. And just to make it even, we could throw occasional hot, albeit *meaningless* sex in there to round things out to an even five "checks". But... considering us anything more than good friends who decided to get married because it was convenient was honestly laughable. That's why it was baffling to me that Adrian actually thought I was going to wait around for him while he served a sentence in *federal prison*.

Like... real ass prison.

That negro was out of his mind.

He waited as long as he possibly could to tell me he was under investigation for securities fraud. He was sweaty, and nervous, and stuttering, and not at all the cool, collected Adrian I knew. I could accept that I'd committed my life to a man who wasn't my "soul mate". I could *not* accept that I'd married a criminal... until the FBI started showing up at the house and freezing our accounts, and news vans started popping up in the front yard. I couldn't really be in denial after *that*, which is why I was preparing to sublet an apartment thousands of miles away, where hardly anybody knew Adrian's name. Here I was, leaving in disgrace, to go back home.

Back home.

Guess how I left home in the first place?

Yep.... *in disgrace.*

I didn't *want* to go home. What I *wanted* to do was throw a fit.

You get what you get, and you don't throw a fit.

I had no idea why *that* kept coming to the forefront of my mind, because if *anybody* deserved to throw a fit... *I* deserved to be throw a fit. And I don't mean a sitting around pouting for a few hours with ice cream and a glass of wine kind of fit. No, I mean a snotty-nosed crying, rolling around on the floor, black auntie at a funeral kind of fit.

FBI, SEC, IRS... I'd dealt with enough abbreviated government agencies to make my head spin by the time they were done tearing our life apart. But once I finally got the news that *I* had been cleared of any wrongdoing... only one acronym mattered.

POS.

No, not *that* one, even though as of late, Adrian was frequently a piece of shit in my thoughts... and words, and emails, and texts, etc. No, the *POS* I refer to is the cute little saying I'd run across in various groups online, for women trying to conceive a baby: peeing on a stick.

I had to make sure that bastard hadn't gotten me pregnant.

Please God, don't let me be pregnant.

That sentiment was a big difference from six or seven months ago, when I actually *wanted* a little blue plus sign to pop up on a plastic stick. I needed *somebody* around here that I could love on. Now, as I stood in the bathroom, furiously washing my hands to pass the time, I wanted nothing more than a big, fat, minus.

If Adrian had finally succeeded at getting me pregnant, after months of trying... I was *gonna* throw that fit.

I somehow found the self-control to not look at the test until the two minutes had passed, then I snatched it from the counter and held it in front of my eyes.

My heart slammed to the front of my chest.

Halle-freakin'-lujah.

I tossed the test into the trashcan with a flourish, and pranced into the bedroom I'd shared with Adrian for the last three years. Before all of the bullshit, this had been a beautiful room, decorated in lush summer blue, gray, and white. Now, all the accessories I'd painstakingly chosen — gorgeous bed linens from Paris, one-of-a-kind paintings commissioned from black artists... everything was packed away in boxes. One set of boxes for the storage building I couldn't really afford, one set marked as "evidence", and one set tagged for auction — to pay restitution to Adrian's victims.

Victims.

I'd married a man who had *victims.*

Kelis' *Caught Out There* cycled through the speakers, and

I cranked it up louder. *"I hate you so much right now"* was a more than appropriate sentiment for the onerous task of clearing out the house — to be sold as well.

"I can't believe you're bailing on me Charlie. I thought we were in this thing together— forever."

Hmph.

The look on Adrian's face when I had to explain that he'd *thought* wrong was comical.

This *entire thing* was.

I almost laughed as I pulled the boxes of ovulation prediction kits from under the bathroom counter, tossing them into the bin marked "purge".

Almost.

Because it wasn't funny, not even a little, that instead of happily planning a baby with my husband, I was packing the wreckage of my life into as few boxes as I could. There was nothing amusing about the hassle of settling massive bills, talking to lawyers, and keeping a tenuous hold on the only thing I had left.

It was messed up.

I was messed up.

Maybe I should be sticking by my husband.

So what that he was kinda... vanilla. He was good to me, and he made me laugh. In general, he was a little on the quiet side, but *so what*? When prodded, the man could talk people, politics, and pop culture, so we were never hard up for conversation. *So what* that we didn't love each other "like that"? Before the decision to get married, we were friends. So maybe... maybe I did love him a little. It wasn't possible to live with someone for three years and not develop a certain level of fondness. Repeatedly, the thought that I could *really* use one of Adrian's firm, delicious-smelling hugs ran through my mind... but, oh, yeah.

Adrian was a POS.

Yeah. *That* kind.

When I boarded that flight to Morocco for our ridiculous, bougie-overload destination wedding, I had no idea that three years later, the man I married would be sitting in a federal prison awaiting trial. *Real ass prison.* Nothing tipped me off that "investment banker" — at least in Adrian's case — was just code for "white collar criminal". There were zero hints that he'd funded our luxurious life on the backs of little old ladies living off their husband's pensions.

His pleas of innocence meant nothing to me when I — and my clients, friends, hell, the *mailman* — was watching dateline-esque probes by the local new station, with my husband's face — and sometimes *mine* — constantly flashed across the screen.

No.

No.

He could talk to me when he'd won an appeal.

My music stopped.

A text message notification interrupted the stream, and I pulled the last of the things under the cabinet out, dumping them in the trash before I went to collect my phone. When I saw the name of the person who'd sent the message, I lifted an eyebrow.

When I *read* the message, I played *Caught Out There* again.

It was even *more* appropriate for *lost his mind negro number two*, on the other end of this text.

I took a deep breath, and ignored his message. I could

deal with *that* later. For now, my priorities were getting this house cleared, and not missing my flight.

The next several hours were devoted to packing the last of our things. Once they were securely taped, and tagged with a prepaid shipping label, the boxes with my personal belongings would go to my cousin's apartment, where I would be staying until I found a place of my own.

Almost too late, I remembered that I needed clothing for the few days it would take to get the boxes cross-country. I found my luggage in a — luckily not-yet-taped — box, and filled my carryon with a random assortment of tee shirts, jeans, and underwear. I didn't anticipate needing or feeling like putting in the effort into looking cute.

The way I saw it, I was in mourning. For my lifestyle, my house, my dignity... and my marriage. None of this was easy for me. I didn't feel brave, or free, or relieved, I felt... like a failure. My grand plan to marry someone who made sense, versus someone who affected my sensibilities... wasn't so grand.

As a last act of wifely benevolence, I packed as many of Adrian's treasured belongings as I could fit into two large boxes, and slapped on a shipping label that would take them to his mother's house. If you wanna talk about a ride-or-die, *that* lady was it. When it came to the men in her life, Sandra Richards believed the sun rose on their whim, and set on their command. She was beyond scandalized that I wasn't visiting Adrian every day, weeping, and lamenting, and decrying the injustice of it all, because *didn't I know her son was innocent,* and *don't you know what you won't do, another woman will.*

Uh, no girl.

The alphabet soup of agencies with Adrian's name at the top of their lists, the fact that even my *personal* assets were frozen, pending investigation, and the fact that he was sitting in federal prison — *real ass prison* — all told a different story about his innocence. I couldn't, and *wouldn't* put my life on hold for that. And as far as another woman taking my please?

Hmph.

She could have his ass.

— & —

BY DESIGN, NO ONE WAS WAITING FOR ME AT THE airport. I didn't want to see *anybody*, I wanted to get to my new apartment, take a long nap, and wake up to realize this was all just a horrible nightmare.

My cousin, who I was subletting from, had already sent me the key, so I let myself in and took in my surroundings. Being back in this city, back in this neighborhood... I'd expected to feel anxious, and maybe even a little afraid. The people I considered my friends before... would they still feel that way? But somehow, as I stepped up to the large window that looked out over familiar streets, I just felt... *home*.

I knew my mother would be ready to kill me for not being the first to know I was back in town, but I wasn't ready to deal with her dramatics. Between her and my aunt Morgan, they probably already had a list of potential *new* husbands waiting for me, and I wasn't quite rid of the first yet.

Instead of calling her — or anyone else — I texted my cousin to let her know I was there, then stripped down to nothing and took a hot shower. It was late, and I was *tired*. After my shower, I crawled into the bed and closed my eyes. *Starting over* could wait until tomorrow.

If you enjoyed this book, please consider leaving a review at your retailer of choice. It doesn't have to be long - just a line or two about why you enjoyed the book, or even a simple star rating can be very helpful for any author!

Want to stay connected? Text 'CCJRomance' to 74121 or sign up for my newsletter. I'll keep you looped into what I'm doing!

Check out CCJROMANCE.COM for first access to all my new releases, signed paperbacks, merch, and more!

I'm all over the social mediasphere - find me everywhere @beingmrsjones

For a full listing of titles by Christina C Jones, visit www.beingmrsjones.com/books

about the author

Christina C. Jones is a best-selling romance novelist and digital media creator. A timeless storyteller, she is lauded by readers for her ability to seamlessly weave the complexities of modern life into captivating tales of Black characters in nearly every romance subgenre. In addition to her full-time writing career, she co-founded Girl, Have You Read – a popular digital platform that amplifies Black romance authors and their stories. Christina has a passion for making beautiful things, and be found crafting, cooking, and designing and building a (literal) home with her husband in her spare time.